The Obsidian Eye

Secret Societies and the Sisterhood Sleuths

Cathy Warshaw

All illustrations (interior) by Oksana Ponomar

ISBN: 979-8-218-99219-4 (paperback)
ISBN: 979-8-218-99220-0 (hardcover)
ISBN: 979-8-89901-761-2 (ebook)

Disclaimer
This book is a work of fiction. While some locations, events, and individuals are inspired by actual events, places, and figures, all characters have been fictionalized. The events depicted in this story are entirely fictional. For all other characters, any resemblance to real persons, living or deceased, is purely coincidental and unintentional.

To my grandchildren,

Morgan, Justin, Elliotte, Alexander, and Zackery

You are my greatest inspiration.
This story is for you, with all my love

To join the

Secret Societies and the Sisterhood Sleuths club

go to

https://www.sisterhoodsleuths.net, or

https://www.sisterhoodsleuths.blog

CONTENTS

Prologue

The morning sun spilled over Upland, California, bathing the town in a golden glow that could have been plucked straight from a postcard. Rows of craftsman homes stood like old friends, their neatly trimmed hedges guarding secrets older than the town itself.

Somewhere, a lawn mower hummed, and the faint scent of citrus from nearby groves wafted through the air. Upland felt like a place where the biggest drama was Mrs. Hargrove's cat refusing to come down from a tree—or so it seemed.

Beneath the perfect façade, the town whispered of mysterious stories most people were either too busy or too afraid to hear. Stories of hidden passageways in grand old mansions, of tunnels that stretched beneath the streets like veins beneath the skin. To most, these tales were merely that—stories but to Chloe and Lily Hastings, they were intriguing puzzles waiting to be solved.

The sisters sat on the front porch of their weathered Victorian house on Lemon Avenue. With its chipped blue paint and creaky steps, the house resembled an eccentric aunt—full of quirks, charm, and a tendency to groan when the wind blew.

Chloe, twenty, leaned casually against the railing, her mid-length blonde hair catching the light like a halo. At 5 foot eight, she had a presence that turned heads, but it wasn't just her looks; it was the way her blue eyes seemed to assess the world, as if she were preparing for a chess match. Her calm, deliberate demeanor often led people to believe she was older than her years, which was fine with Chloe. It meant fewer people asked annoying questions.

Beside her, Lily was a whirlwind of activity, perched cross-legged on the porch swing with a sketchpad precariously balanced on her knees. At eighteen, she was five foot five, with long brown hair that refused to be tamed, no matter how many brushes or elastics she tried to use. Her hazel eyes sparkled with ideas as her pencil darted across the page. Lily was the kind of person who could sketch a dragon mid-flight while simultaneously humming off-key to a song stuck in her head. Her boundless energy perfectly countered Chloe's methodical approach.

"You're doing it again," Lily said, not bothering to look up from her work.

"Doing what?" Chloe replied, not even glancing in her direction.

"Don't overthink it; you might hurt yourself."

Chloe rolled her eyes but didn't argue. Her younger sister wasn't wrong. For months, one thing had consumed her mind: **The Society.**

At first, the rumors about The Society had seemed like just another oddity of Upland—a town rich in folklore and half-truths. However, the more Chloe and Lily explored, the more real the whispers became. Those who asked too many questions suddenly relocated or completely vanished.

And now, the sisters had their own questions.

"It doesn't fit," Chloe muttered.

"What doesn't?" Lily asked, pausing her sketching.

Before Chloe could respond, laughter rang out down the street. A group of kids on bikes sped by, their voices carefree and loud. It was the kind of sound that made Upland feel alive, as if the world were full of possibilities. But for Chloe and Lily, it reminded them how much they had to lose. Upland wasn't just a town; it was home.

Now ... *it was in danger.*

Their sleuthing journey had started with small puzzles—missing heirlooms, playful school pranks, and the occasional town mystery that sparked their curiosity. Lately, however, they were finding themselves more deeply involved, pursuing a shadowy organization that appeared to be everywhere yet remained just out of reach.

The resulting tension between them had snapped like a rubber band earlier, when Chloe, her eyes wide, had handed Lily a crumpled envelope. It had been sitting there that morning, wedged beneath the front door. There was no stamp, no address, just one word scrawled across the front: **HASTINGS.**

Inside had been a grainy photograph of the two of them, taken from outside their window. With it was a note written in bold black ink:

Stop looking.

For a moment, neither sister had said a word. The weight of the warning between them thick, like the humid air before a storm.

Lily had broken the silence. "Well, that's not ominous or anything."

Chloe pressed her lips into a thin line, hardened her eyes, and shook her head. "We'll keep looking."

Lily had flashed that reckless smile that always made Chloe wonder whether her sister was fearless or simply bad at assessing risk. "Of course we do. Who do they think they're dealing with?"

Now, sitting together on the porch, Lily put her sketchpad down and smiled gently. "Together?" Lily asked, her hand softly resting on Chloe's arm.

"Always," Chloe replied, her tone firm.

The sun was getting lower in the sky, casting long shadows that stretched toward the sisters like outstretched fingers. Somewhere in the distance, a wind chime played its cheerful tune—a stark contrast to the unease creeping up their spines.

Upland may have seemed like the perfect town, but Chloe and Lily were aware of the truth. Behind the well-kept lawns and sunlit streets, something sinister was lurking—something they were determined to uncover.

With that, the sisters stepped off the porch together, prepared to confront whatever lurked in the shadows.

Chapter 1

The Unexpected Invitation

Have you ever experienced something so strange that it felt as if the universe had shifted just for you? That's exactly what happened to Chloe and Lily Hastings on a crisp autumn afternoon. The air was cool and filled with the scent of fallen leaves, as they walked home. It was the kind of afternoon when the ordinary seemed to hum with possibility.

Their path wound past the Madonna of the Trail, a weathered stone statue that stood as the town's silent sentinel. Chloe, ever the dreamer, paused as they walked by, her eyes lingering on the figure. She had always imagined it held secrets hidden away in its cold stone heart—secrets of the past, whispered to anyone daring enough to listen.

"I bet she's seen it all," Chloe mused, brushing a strand of blonde hair from her face. "Wars, peace, scandals …"

"Don't forget those awkward small-town dances," Lily quipped, her eyes sparkling with mischief. At eighteen, she had a knack for making every moment feel lighthearted. "Whether she's a statue or not, she'd probably agree that our town's biggest mystery is whether the bakery's muffins are truly homemade."

Chloe rolled her eyes but smiled. "You lack imagination."

"You definitely have way too much of it," Lily joked, giving her sister's shoulder a playful nudge.

When they arrived home, the last thing they expected was the thick envelope lying on their doorstep. Its cream-colored paper gleamed softly in the late afternoon light, looking like something from another era. Chloe bent down to pick it up, holding it carefully as if it might burst into flames.

"Who still uses envelopes like this?" she wondered, flipping it over. There was no return address—only their last name, *Hastings*, elegantly written in black script.

"That's … ominous," Lily said, glancing over Chloe's shoulder. "So? Go ahead and open it!"

Chloe hesitated her cautious instincts on high alert. That earlier letter earlier had been a warning. "What if it's a prank? Or something even more dangerous?"

Lily grabbed the envelope before Chloe could object. "There's only one way to find out." With a dramatic gesture, she tore it open.

Inside, there was an invitation embossed in gold letters so shiny they almost glowed:

To Chloe and Lily Hastings,

You are officially invited to the Gala at Sycamore Estates this Saturday at 8 PM. A car will come to escort you. Please dress appropriately.

There was no signature, no explanation—just those tantalizing, mysterious words.

"Sycamore Estates?" Lily's voice rose with excitement. "That's *the* gala, Chloe. The one everyone talks about all year. Only VIPs get invited—like, the VIPs of town *royalty*." Her fingers made air quotes on the word.

Chloe frowned as she read the card again. "But … why us? We're not exactly 'royalty.'"

"Maybe someone noticed our detective skills," Lily said, wiggling her eyebrows. "We're somewhat famous for solving that whole missing cat-and-diamond-earring fiasco."

"Or it's a trap," Chloe said flatly as she placed the invitation on the kitchen counter. "This is too random. Too … strange."

The sisters spent the evening locked in debate. Chloe paced back and forth, detailing every potential danger. "What if it's a trap? What if we show up and find ourselves in some bizarre movie-villain scenario? Like … I don't know … sharks with lasers?"

Lily, sprawled out on her bed, brushed aside her sister's worries. "You've been watching too many spy movies. Just think about it—this is our chance! A fancy gala, an exclusive crowd … If there's a mystery, it's practically begging us to solve it."

"And what if it's not? What if we're heading into trouble we can't handle?" Chloe replied sharply.

"Then we prepare," Lily said, sitting up with newfound determination. "We'll research the estate, figure out who's hosting, and—"

"Let's make a *plan*," Chloe interrupted, her frown softening. Despite her reluctance, she felt a flicker of curiosity. "Okay. But we're doing this my way. No improvising."

"Deal," Lily said with a smile, extending her pinky finger.

Chloe sighed and linked pinkies with her sister. "You're impossible."

"And you love me for it."

By the time they went to bed, the invitation rested between their desks, drawing their thoughts like a magnet toward the unknown. Whatever awaited them at Sycamore Estates would not be ordinary. It was a doorway they were both excited to step through in their own way.

The gala was more than just an event; it marked the start of a story they never realized they were going to play a big role in.

Chapter 2

Whispered Secrets of Upland

The morning sun filtered through the lace curtains of their shared bedroom, casting a soft, golden glow over the cluttered space. Chloe's side of the room was a chaotic mix of open notebooks, highlighters, and a laptop that was always running low on battery. Watercolor palettes and unfinished sketches sprawled across every available surface of Lily's side.

"You really need to clean up," Lily joked, flicking an eraser at Chloe.

Chloe sat cross-legged on the rug, her gaze fixed downward. "I'm organizing. There's a difference." She tucked a strand of blonde hair behind her ear, her eyes focused on a map of Upland.

"We should begin with the library," she stated, her voice sharp. "If The Society is tied to this gala, there has to be something in the records. They've been lurking in the shadows of this town for decades, maybe even longer."

"Did you know that the Madonna of the Trail is believed to mark a concealed entrance to the tunnels?" Lily exclaimed, flipping through a book on local legends. "It's just a rumor, but imagine if it were true."

"Rumors are like glitter," Chloe said. "They cling to everything but don't really offer any assistance."

Lily rolled her hazel eyes. "You're no fun."

The banter continued as they walked to the Upland Public Library, which smelled of aged paper and echoed with hushed voices. Behind the desk stood Evelyn Greene, a lively librarian whose silver-rimmed glasses and perpetually messy bun gave her the impression of someone who belonged in a mystery novel.

"Ah, the Hastings sisters," Evelyn said with a warm greeting. "What kind of trouble are you getting into today?"

Chloe smiled. "I'm researching Upland, particularly The Society."

Evelyn's smile faded. She leaned in closer, her voice dropping to a whisper. "That's not something you research lightly."

"But you know something about them," Lily urged, her curiosity piqued, sparking like a flash and ready to ignite.

Evelyn hesitated, scanning the room to make sure they were alone. At last, she motioned for them to follow her. "Come with me and keep quiet."

She led them to a small, dusty room at the back of the library, filled with shelves of worn books, ancient maps, and newspapers too fragile to handle without care. On the central oak table lay peculiar objects: a magnifying glass, a brass device resembling a combination lock, and a quill pen that seemed to belong in a Victorian drama.

"This is where Upland hides its secrets," Evelyn said. "If you want answers, you'll need to solve the puzzles first."

Chloe's gaze focused on a faded note lying among the papers. She picked it up and read aloud:

"The key to the hidden door lies where words align.
The second letter of the first, the third of the second, and so on.
Only when the message is complete will the path reveal itself.
Begin where the past meets the present."

"What does that mean?" Lily asked, furrowing her brow.

"It's a cipher," Evelyn explained. "A puzzle. The instructions are clear, but solving it will require some thought."

The sisters shared an eager glance. "Let's do this," Chloe said, already scanning the room.

The Puzzle Hunt

She moved first to the sturdy oak table in the center of the room, where the brass combination lock lay incongruously amidst a collection of dusty antiques. She picked it up, noticing that the numbers on its face were faded but still legible—1882. Evelyn watched silently, her expression giving nothing away.

"1882," Chloe murmured, turning it over in her hands. "That's not random. It's the year Upland was founded. Maybe it points us toward something historical?"

Lily darted toward a nearby bookshelf labeled Local History, her fingertips tracing the worn spines as she searched for the right book. "Here it is! 'Founding of Upland: A Complete History.'"

She quickly pulled it from the shelf and flipped it open. Loose pages fluttered to the floor, revealing a small, hand-drawn map tucked between the old, yellowed sheets. She picked it up carefully, turning it over to reveal letters scribbled hastily in faded ink: L-N.

"L-N?" Lily asked aloud, turning back to her sister. "What could that mean?"

"Landmarks?" Chloe suggested, coming closer. "Or initials of someone important from Upland's history?" She examined the map carefully. "L-N … wait, Lily, do you remember Grandma's stories? She spoke about Lillian North and her writings about Upland's history."

Lily's eyes brightened instantly. "You're right! She always loved those old books. Maybe we're supposed to look for something written by Lillian North?"

Chloe smiled for a moment. "Also, the clue mentioned 'where words align.' North was a poet as well as a historian. Let's check her poems?"

Lily hurried toward the poetry anthology shelf, looking over the spines until she stopped at a collection of poems by Lillian North. Carefully pulling it out, she opened it to find certain words clearly highlighted.

"Chloe, look!" Lily exclaimed excitedly, holding up the open pages. "The bold letters spell something out: H-I-D-D-E-N." Chloe repeated softly, "Hidden … what's hidden? Where?"

Their eyes moved simultaneously toward the antique oak table at the room's center. In the fairly modern library, the table looked out of place, especially with the odd items on its surface.

Evelyn stood still, just watching them as the sisters hurried to the table and began to run their fingers along its carved edges. Chloe made a small noise, drawing Lily's attention. She had suddenly noticed a small, concealed drawer just beneath the surface. She pulled it open carefully, revealing another slip of paper with letters spelling out D-O-O-R.

"Hidden door," Lily breathed, eyes wide.

"It's coming together. We know what we're looking for now, Lily … start on the other side of the room and look for any part of the wall that's a bit weird," Chloe breathed, scanning the room.

The Secret Room

For a long time, while Evelyn patiently observed, the sisters examined every wall surface carefully. Then Chloe felt slight irregularities in the wood paneling beside a bookshelf. "Lily! I think this is it."

Her sister quickly moved to her side as she traced a faint indentation almost invisible to the naked eye. With nary a thought about caution, she pressed firmly against the spot.

A faint click echoed softly, and a subtle seam widened, outlining a narrow door concealed in the wall. "I found it," Chloe whispered excitedly.

They slowly pushed the door open, revealing a dark passageway lined with cobwebs and damp stone walls stretching into darkness.

At the end of the passage stood an ornate wooden door, intricately carved with symbols of stars and interlocking circles. Chloe pressed a brass plaque in the center, causing the door to creak open and unveil a hidden archive. The room was spacious and dimly lit. Its walls were decorated with maps, charts, and mysterious documents. At the center stood a mahogany desk cluttered with files and a glowing, spinning globe that hummed softly.

"Check this out," Lily whispered, her eyes wide as she picked up a folder labeled *Jerusalem Protocol.* Inside, there was a stack of papers—diagrams, notes scribbled in the margins, photographs of various sites, some ancient,
some well-known, others just plain mysterious.

"What is all this?" Chloe said, leaning in. "It looks like plans to manipulate archaeological findings or something. Was whoever left these wanting to falsify history?"

Chloe flipped through another file. "Delphi Initiative … Kyoto Nexus … Varanasi Accord … This isn't merely a local conspiracy. It's global. They're staging discoveries."

Lily turned to her. "Why would The Society need to alter archaeological evidence?"

"Power." Chloe replied. "I cannot think of anything else."

On the desk, the glowing globe cast the image of a web of connections across the world against the opposite wall. Chloe traced the lines with her finger, her voice barely above a whisper. "They've woven in their influence everywhere."

Then, Lily picked up a notebook. Within it, she discovered a drawing of a black gemstone—the caption read 'The Obsidian Eye'—paired with the words: *The Eye sees all. When the circles align, it begins.*

Faint footsteps echoed down the hallway before they could fully process everything they had seen.

"They know we're here," Evelyn whispered. "We have to leave. Now."

Hastily picking up as many papers and things as they could carry, the sisters and Evelyn slipped back into the passage, their minds racing with the implications of what they had uncovered—and the clear danger now closing in around them.

Chapter 3

The Great Escape to Safe Haven

The faint sound of footsteps echoed ominously down the corridor, growing louder with each passing second. Chloe, Lily, and Evelyn froze, their breaths shallow, their eyes darting toward the shadows creeping along the walls.

"They're coming," Evelyn whispered, clutching a rolled-up map to her chest nervously. Her face was ashen and her voice trembled. "We have to get out of here."

Chloe nodded, her heart racing. "Let's head back the way we came—"

"No," Evelyn hissed, her gaze darting to a narrow doorway at the far end of the concealed room. "If they see the passage open, they'll know someone's been here. We'll need to find another way."

Lily's voice was a squeak as panic set in. "Another

way? What if there's none?"

Chloe swallowed hard, urging herself to sound calm. She held her sister's hand, providing a reassuring squeeze despite her clammy palms. "We'll figure it out," she said. "Come on."

Evelyn led the way, guiding them through the doorway. The new corridor was narrow and lined with dead torches covered in cobwebs, their wooden handles aged and cracked. The air grew colder with each step, sending chills down their spines as the flashlight's dim beam flickered over the uneven stone floor.

Behind them, the muffled voices of their pursuers grew louder, splitting off in different directions. Chloe's stomach twisted as her mind raced. *How did they know to look for us? Were they tracking us somehow?* She pushed those thoughts aside; there was no time to think of answers now.

"They're spreading out," Evelyn murmured, glancing back over her shoulder. "They'll search both paths."

Lily groaned softly. "Wonderful. Now we'll be stuck."

"Not if we keep moving," Chloe said, her voice laced with false confidence. She couldn't allow her fear to show—especially not now. "Just stay close."

The corridor ended suddenly at a solid brick wall. Lily's breath caught as she looked back at the advancing torchlight. "This is it. We're done."

"No, we're not," Chloe replied sharply. Her gaze swept the wall, noticing faint etchings on the bricks—symbols carved into the stone. They seemed oddly familiar.

"The sequence from the globe," she said, recalling as the memory clicked into place. "The map projections weren't just connections—they were instructions!"

"What sequence?" Evelyn asked, her voice rising in pitch as the shouts of the pursuit grew nearer.

Chloe pressed her fingers against the bricks, tracing the familiar pattern: a compass-like shape starting at the north point. Her heart raced as she pressed the last brick. The wall trembled before sliding open with a low rumble, revealing a sloping tunnel.

"This way!" Chloe whispered urgently, pulling Lily and Evelyn through just as the torchlight illuminated the now vacant corridor. The wall closed behind them with a quiet thud, sealing off their pursuers.

They stood in the dark tunnel, breathing heavily. Chloe felt her knees starting to buckle, but she forced herself to stand tall. She wasn't going to let Lily see her break down.

"That was too close," Lily muttered, clutching the stolen files tightly to her chest. Her voice trembled, but a faint smile curled at her lips. "Nice job, Sherlock."

Chloe smirked, the tension easing a bit. "Thanks, Watson. Now let's get out of here."

There was a rusted metal grate at the end of the tunnel which Chloe quickly opened. They stepped out into a dense grove of trees, just beyond the library's grounds. The cool, crisp night air, fragrant with eucalyptus, hit them with a jolt.

"We can't stay here," Evelyn said, glancing back at the towering silhouette of the library. Behind its shadowy windows, figures moved, and faint voices shouted commands. Her tone was sharp, but a flicker of something in her eyes—regret perhaps—suggested deeper emotions. "They'll search the area once they realize we're gone."

"So, where do we go?" Lily asked, scanning the empty streets of Upland in the distance. Her voice cracked with exhaustion. "We can't go home—they may know where we live if they suspect it was us—and we can't just … roam around."

Chloe spread the map Evelyn had taken. Her gaze was fixed on a small circle just outside the city. Next to it, the words *Safe Haven—1947* were scribbled in faded ink.

"What's this?" Chloe asked, raising the map for Evelyn to see.

Evelyn's expression grew serious. "A place I've only heard whispers of. If it still exists, it could be our only chance at the moment. But …"

"But what?" Lily pressed.

Evelyn hesitated, clutching the flashlight tightly. "The Society used it once," she admitted. "And they might still be keeping an eye on it."

Chloe and Lily exchanged a glance. What next?

The trio moved through the dark streets of Upland, staying in the shadows. Chloe's heart raced at every rustling leaf or distant car engine, but she maintained her focus. Lily held the files tightly, while Evelyn examined the map, her flashlight dimmed to avoid detection.

As they approached the city's outskirts, the lights faded into rolling hills and thick groves of lemon trees. Evelyn halted at an overgrown path, partially hidden by thorny bushes.

"This is it," she said, stepping onto the trail.

The path wound upward, flanked by ancient oaks with gnarled branches reaching for the moonlit sky. At the summit of the hill, they discovered it: a crumbling stone structure, overrun by ivy. The weathered doors hung slightly ajar, creaking as Evelyn pushed them open.

The interior was cold and damp, filled with mildew and a musty scent permeating the air. Moonlight filtered through broken windows, illuminating a vast room adorned with faded murals of constellations, cryptic symbols, and a solitary, haunting image of an eye encircled by radiating lines.

"The Obsidian Eye," Chloe murmured, gazing at the mural. Her chest tightened as though the painted eye could see right through her. "Why does it feel like it's watching us?"

Walking to the center of the room, Evelyn wiped the dust off a table in the center of the room. Its surface was marked with coordinates, Latin phrases, and intricate diagrams. "This wasn't just a hideout," she observed. "It was a war room."

Lily knelt beside a small iron handle embedded in the floor. "What's this?"

Chloe joined her, pulling it open to reveal a ladder that led down into darkness. A shiver ran down her spine. "Of course, there would be a creepy underground section."

"Stay close," Evelyn said as they went down.

The chamber below was smaller but meticulously organized. Shelves lined the walls, filled with journals, maps, and ledgers. At the center stood a pedestal holding a black gemstone intricately carved with symbols, which shimmered faintly in the dim light.

"Is that ... the Obsidian Eye?" Lily asked softly.

Evelyn's expression grew serious. "A replica. If the real one is as powerful as they say, it could affect everything—people, events, even history."

Chloe scanned a journal on the shelf and froze. "These plans ... They're experiments. Propaganda, psychological manipulation … They were fighting dirty."

Evelyn hesitated. "Desperation can blur the lines, but what matters now is understanding how they battled and what we can learn from it."

A faint creak from a door broke the silence above them. Chloe felt a chill run down her spine.

"They found us," she whispered.

Evelyn extinguished the flashlight. "Hide. Now."

As they scrambled for cover, Chloe's mind raced. If they survived this, they would need more than luck—they would need answers. The sound of footsteps echoed down the ladder, and a shadow loomed at the top of the steps, growing larger as it began to descend.

Chapter 4

Unexpected Ally

The silhouette at the top of the ladder danced and twisted as footsteps softly echoed through the chamber. Chloe's heart was pounding so hard she was afraid it would give them away. She tightened her grip on Lily's hand, their breaths just shallow gasps as they huddled together behind a rusty set of shelves. Just ahead, Evelyn stood determinedly, her knuckles white around the metal rod she had found, ready for whatever lay ahead.

A calm voice eased the tension. "I'm not here to hurt you." It was a man's voice, low and steady, with a faint Middle Eastern accent. "If you're against The Society, we're on the same side."

Chloe glanced at Evelyn, whose lips formed a thin, skeptical line. With careful movements, Evelyn stepped into the light of flashlight Chloe had switched on. The

The rod remained firmly in her grip

"Who are you?" Evelyn demanded.

A man stepped into the beam of the flashlight. He seemed to be in his late twenties, his dark, wavy hair a bit tousled as if he had just come from a storm. A neatly trimmed beard framed his face, and his brown eyes scanned the room with a focus that made Chloe shiver. He wore a leather jacket over a plain cotton shirt, and a laptop bag hung diagonally across his chest, its worn strap showing years of use.

"Gil," he said calmly, raising his hands in a gesture of peace. "I've been tracking The Society for years. When I noticed the activity here tonight, I thought I'd look into it."

"How can we be sure you aren't one of them?" Chloe stepped closer, her eyes sharp and unwavering.

Gil let out a dry chuckle. "If I were, would I have introduced myself? Trust me, I've seen what they do to those who cross them. Being here and talking to you puts everything at risk."

Evelyn lowered her rod by an inch, her eyes still narrowing with scrutiny. "Why are you following The Society?"

"Because they aren't just pulling strings," Gil said, his tone darkening. "They're tying the world into knots—financial systems, resources, communications. Everything is at stake. Their endgame is total control. No government or individual will stand a chance."

Lily, who had been silent until now, frowned. "But why would anyone desire that kind of power?"

"Because they think they're the only ones who can 'fix' the world," Gil's voice dripped with disdain. "They call it The Alignment. It's not about influence; it's about reshaping the world in their image. And people like us? We don't fit into their plan."

The words lingered in the air like smoke. Chloe looked at Evelyn, who appeared to be absorbing its gravity.

"You know a lot about them," Evelyn finally said.

Gil shrugged slightly. "I should. I've spent five years in Upland gathering intelligence. This town is more important to them than anyone realizes. Tunnels, old records, energy lines … Upland is a hub. I've been putting it all together."

"And now you're here," Chloe said, skeptically. "Why?"

Gil's expression softened, but his voice carried a firm resolve. "I can't tackle this alone. Tonight, I saw people who clearly need our support. If we combine our efforts, we might actually have a chance. But we can't stay here; they'll come back. And when they do, we all risk becoming targets."

"What's your plan?" Evelyn asked, stepping closer.

"There's a safehouse, a hidden base. We regroup there, share resources, and plan our next move," Gil said, his eyes scanning their faces. "It's your decision, but I'm offering you a lifeline. Take it."

The sisters exchanged a long glance. Finally, Chloe nodded. "We don't have a choice. Lead the way."

Going to the Safehouse

They worked quickly, sifting through piles of documents and collecting only the essential files and maps to take with them. Gil then led them to a secondary tunnel he had discovered weeks earlier when on a reconnaissance mission. The passage was narrow, forcing them to walk in single file, the walls scraping against their shoulders.

"Stay close," Gil whispered, his voice steady but urgent. "They'll be patrolling soon."

The group stepped out into a lush grove, where the fresh night air welcomed them with the delightful scents of lemons and damp earth. Gil crouched down, scanning the horizon carefully with a clearly well-trained eye. Satisfied, he motioned for everyone to join him.

The trail twisted like a labyrinth through the hills, their breath creating small visible puffs in the chilly air. By the time they arrived at the safe house—a small cabin tucked between two imposing boulders—their legs were sore.

"Here you go," Gil said, unlocking the door. "It may not be much, but it's safe."

Inside, the cabin was surprisingly well-equipped. Monitors and computers hummed softly along one wall. A sturdy wooden table covered with maps and documents dominated the center of the room. The faint scent of coffee and worn leather lingered in the air.

Chloe looked around the space, feeling impressed despite herself. "Is this your base?"

"One of them," Gil said with a wry smile. "Make yourself comfortable. We need to go through those files before my team arrives."

Evelyn was already laying out papers on the table, focusing intensely. "We'll figure this out."

Lily sat beside Chloe, her eyes shining with determination. "This is it, right? The real fight."

Chloe nodded, the old spark of determination igniting in her chest. "Yeah. It is."

Outside, the wind picked up, rustling the trees with an eerie insistence—a quiet warning of the approaching storm.

Chapter 5

More Allies Arrive

The wind howled outside, rattling the cabin's windows as though it were announcing the arrival of something—or someone—momentous. Chloe, Lily, and Evelyn huddled around the large oak table, scattered with files and maps. Their minds raced, even though they were exhausted after the earlier escape and now going over all they had found, added to what was already there in the safehouse.

Chloe turned to Gil, asking, "So, you said you've been following The Society for some years. What do you do exactly?"

Gil stood up and paced slowly as he thought of how to respond. "I'm something of an intelligence analyst," he began, addressing the trio. "I've spent years decoding hidden networks, tracking clandestine financial streams, and unearthing secrets people would rather bury." He gestured toward the table. "This—unraveling the inner workings of The Society—is what I do. They've been controlling information flows, global markets, and even political events. That's my expertise."

As he finished speaking, a sharp knock on the door startled them, piercing the cabin's tense silence.

Gil approached the door with a calm efficiency that seemed to define him. He paused just long enough to look outside. A brief exchange of whispered words followed before he stepped back, his expression a blend of relief and determination.

"This is Thalia," he said, stepping aside to reveal a striking woman with a commanding presence. Her angular features framed sharp green eyes that seemed to notice everything. She carried herself like someone who clearly knew how to manage chaos.

As Thalia entered, the firelight reflected off the silver streak in her jet-black hair. "I hope you have something challenging for me," she said, her voice rich with a melodic Greek accent. "The more difficult the puzzle, the more satisfying the victory."

"Chloe, Lily, Evelyn," Gil said, waving his hand toward them. "Meet the best cryptographer and expert in ancient languages I've ever worked with."

Lily, always quick to ease the tension, gave a small wave. "So, you're like a real-life Indiana Jones?"

Thalia's lips curled into a faint smile. "Without the hat, but with better results."

Before anyone could respond, a second knock sounded. Gil opened the door again to reveal a wiry man in a scuffed leather jacket, his curly black hair swept awry by the wind. He held a sleek tablet under one arm, its edges glowing faintly as if the device itself were eager to be useful.

"This is Raj," Gil said, stepping aside. "He's from India. If The Society has advanced technology—and they always do—he's the one who will discover, disarm or decode it."

Raj flashed a grin so wide it could light up the room. "The fun part isn't breaking their systems," he said as he settled into a chair. "It's watching them scramble to figure out how I did it. Nice to meet you all."

"Do you always bring your own light show?" Chloe asked, gesturing toward his tablet.

"Only when I'm showing off," he said with a wink, prompting a laugh from Lily. Chloe, who was harder to impress, crossed her arms but couldn't hide a small smile.

The door knocked again, and this time, figures entered in a steady flow. Each arrival added a new layer of intrigue and energy to the cabin.

The Team Assembles

Yuki entered next, her petite frame dwarfed by the large duffel she carried. She nodded politely to the group but spoke little, her sharp eyes scanning the room as if she were memorizing it. When Gil introduced her as an engineer specializing in robotics and nanotechnology, Lily leaned over to Chloe and whispered, "She has that 'quiet genius' vibe, doesn't she?"

Mei followed closely behind, her confidence evident in the way she strode in, grasping a clipboard filled with handwritten notes and diagrams. Her background as a biologist and chemist was reflected in the careful precision of her movements. "If The Society is messing with biology, they're amateurs compared to me," she said, setting her clipboard down with a flourish.

Luca's arrival brought a whole new energy. He strolled in as if he owned the place, his Italian accent making every word sound like a secret worth keeping. "Luca," he said, his playful grin as engaging as his overwhelming confidence. "Cybersecurity extraordinaire. If it's locked, I'll unlock it. If it's hidden, I'll find it. And if it's boring, I'll spice it up."

"And if it's dangerous?" Chloe asked dryly.

"Then it's my specialty."

The last two arrivals towered over everyone else. Aoife, broad-shouldered and sporting a weathered face that hinted at long days spent outdoors, introduced herself in a thick Irish brogue that felt warm despite her serious tone. "I'll help you find what they don't want you to see," she said, her gaze lingering on the maps spread out across the table.

Einar, stoic and quiet, had a presence that made even the room feel smaller. He spoke softly, his Icelandic accent lending a sense of certainty to his words. "The Society thinks it can manipulate the Earth itself," he said. "But the Earth has its own way of fighting back. I'll show you how."

The Briefing

As the team settled in, the cabin buzzed with a quiet sense of purpose. Gil stood in the center, his calm voice drawing everyone into focus. "The Society's plans are larger than we realized. These files," he gestured toward the clutter on the table, "point to a global strategy called The Alignment. It's a network of control—economics, technology, environment, you name it. They're connecting everything to ensure no one can stop them."

"That's ambitious," Raj said, his tone a blend of admiration and caution.

"More like terrifying," Chloe muttered.

"Exactly," Gil continued. "But we have an opportunity. Each of you holds a part of the solution. Thalia, you'll decode the maps and files. Raj and Luca, identify their technological weaknesses. Yuki, determine how to bypass their physical systems. Mei, Aoife, and Einar, we need your expertise on the effects on the environment and biology."

"What about us?" Chloe asked, gesturing to herself, Lily, and Evelyn.

"Stay close," Gil said. "You've already uncovered more than anyone expected. Help when you can but be careful. The Society knows who you are now."

The Gala Invitation

Chloe hesitated, feeling the weight of everyone's eyes upon her. She reached into her bag and carefully drew out the elegant envelope, its embossed gold letters catching the dim glow of the cabin's lights.

"There's something else," she began, taking the invitation out of its envelope. "We received this today. It's an invitation—to a gala at Sycamore Estates."

A hush fell over the room, broken only by the soft rustling of paper as Chloe placed the invitation on the table.

"It was delivered anonymously," she continued. "No sender, no details, just instructions." The gala appeared to shift the energy in the room. Raj examined the paper, Luca opened his laptop, and Thalia narrowed her eyes in thought.

"This feels like a trap," Raj said, but excitement laced his voice.

"Or maybe it's an opportunity," Thalia replied. "These events are exactly where The Society operates. Blend in, gather intelligence, and get out before they realize you're there."

"Do we have anything to wear to the gala?" Lily whispered to Chloe, who simply shrugged.

"We'll make do," Chloe said, despite the knot of nerves twisting in her stomach. However, as the team began to plan surveillance, escape routes, and what methods to use to gather information, she couldn't shake the flicker of hope.

The stars outside appeared to shine brighter as the cabin hummed with determination. Whatever lay ahead, they weren't alone anymore.

Chapter 6

Gowns, Gadgets, and Courage

The morning sun poured through the bay windows of the sisters' cozy living room, casting golden rays across the polished hardwood floor. Chloe and Lily sat cross-legged on a soft, cream-colored rug, surrounded by a scattered collection of makeup palettes, curling irons, and shimmering dresses draped over every available surface. The aroma of freshly brewed coffee drifted in from the kitchen, mingling with the soothing lavender scent of a flickering candle.

"Do you think this is too much?" Lily asked, holding an emerald-green gown against her petite frame. She tilted her head, examining herself in the mirror as the fabric caught the light like a liquid jewel.

Chloe glanced up, skillfully winding a section of her blonde hair around a curling iron. "Too much? Lil, it's a gala, not a gym class. If you're not sparkling, you're doing it wrong."

Lily snorted, tossing the dress onto the back of the couch. "Easy for you to say, Miss 'Effortlessly Glamorous.' It's just … surreal. A week ago, we were sneaking into dusty libraries and chasing rumors. Now, we're about to walk into a room potentially full of members of a secret society. What if we mess it up?"

Chloe set the curling iron down, her eyes locking with Lily's in the mirror. "We're not letting this opportunity slip away. We've got this. And besides, we're not in this alone anymore." She pointed to the coffee table, where her phone buzzed with a notification from Gil: *Security on-site is tight. Text me if you need backup. Stay safe.*

Lily glanced at the screen and gave a faint smile. "It's strange, isn't it? Being part of this … team. It feels like we truly belong to something bigger."

Chloe nodded, a faint smile tugging at her lips. "Grandma would be so proud of us."

"Yeah," Lily agreed, her voice now softer. "She'd probably be in the kitchen, baking cookies for us to sneak in."

"Her famous chocolate chip cookies," Chloe said with nostalgically. "And Dad would walk around, lecturing us about 'using our heads and trusting our instincts.'"

Lily's smile dimmed a little. "Do you think he would be okay with us getting involved in this?"

Chloe walked across the room and sat next to her sister. "Dad always said to stand up for what's right, even when it's scary. He'd be worried, sure, but he'd be proud of us." She squeezed Lily's hand in reassurance.

Lily swallowed hard, her eyes sparkling. Then, she jumped to her feet and grabbed the emerald dress. "Alright, emerald-green it is." She slipped it on, spinning dramatically. "How do I look?"

Chloe grinned, grabbing her phone to snap a picture. "Like a movie star about to win an award." She handed Lily the phone. "Now zip me into mine, and don't mess up my hair. I have a reputation to uphold."

Laughter filled the room as they fell into a familiar rhythm, supporting each other in perfecting every detail. Chloe's deep midnight-blue dress hugged her slim frame beautifully, while Lily's gown showcased her youthful energy with its bold, shimmering tones.

By late afternoon, they stood side by side in front of the mirror, scrutinizing their appearance, a mix of anticipation and nerves visible on their faces.

"Do you think we'll discover who's responsible for all this tonight?" Lily asked, her voice barely above a whisper.

Chloe met her own gaze in the mirror. "Maybe. But even if we don't, tonight is about showing them we're not afraid. We're watching, and we won't back down."

Lily nodded, her face displaying fierce determination. "Absolutely. There's no turning back."

As the clock struck five, they gathered their essentials: tiny clutch purses, a notebook disguised as a makeup compact, and the miniature recording device Raj had lent them. Chloe frowned as she turned the device over, noticing a faint scratch on its side. "Weird," she murmured, gently shaking it.

"What?" Lily asked, slipping on her heels.

"Nothing," Chloe said, brushing it off. "It's probably fine."

The soft hum of an engine outside drew their attention. A sleek black sedan rolled up to the curb, its tinted windows glinting in the fading sunlight.

Chloe grasped her sister's hand, a playful grin spreading across her face. "Ready to crash the party, partner?"

Lily laughed, linking arms with her. "Always."

The cool evening air enveloped them as they stepped onto the pavement. A slight shiver of unease prickled at the back of Lily's neck, but she brushed it aside. With Gil's texts, Yuki's layout of the gala venue embedded firmly in her memory, and the rest of the team on standby, they weren't facing this alone.

As the driver opened the car door for them, Chloe leaned in closer. "No matter what happens, we have each other, okay?"

Lily nodded, her voice steady. "Always."

With that, the sisters climbed into the car, leaving the warmth of their home behind.

Chapter 7

The Gala

The sleek black sedan glided silently up the long, winding driveway of the Sycamore Estate. Outside, strands of twinkling lights wrapped around the towering sycamore trees, their golden glow reflecting off the polished car. Chloe and Lily leaned forward together, their faces close to the tinted windows as the sprawling mansion emerged from the darkness like something out of a movie.

"It's even more intimidating in person," Lily whispered, clutching the edges of her emerald green dress.

"Exactly as I imagined," Chloe replied, her voice steady despite the tension in her shoulders. Her eyes scanned the scene—a sea of elegant guests in sparkling gowns and tailored suits mingling around the grand entrance. "It's just a big house, Lil. We can handle this."

The car came to a stop, and a uniformed driver stepped out, opening the doors. The cool night air rushed in as Chloe and Lily stepped onto the cobblestone driveway, their heels clicking sharply against the stones. Chloe's midnight-blue gown shimmered under the golden light, while Lily's dress seemed to glow, its emerald hues providing a striking contrast to the dark night.

"Showtime," Chloe whispered, offering Lily a quick smile as they climbed the broad stone steps toward the massive oak doors.

The mansion's interior was even more breathtaking than its exterior. An enormous crystal chandelier hung from the high ceiling, its prisms scattering rainbows across the polished marble floors. Guests floated through the room, champagne flutes in hand, their conversations blending with the soft strains of a string quartet nestled in one corner. Waiters glided between them, balancing silver trays laden with hors d'oeuvres.

Lily let out a soft whistle. "Alright, I'll admit it. This is a bit … overwhelming."

Chloe's lips curled into a smirk. "Lying to Grandma about sneaking out was overwhelming. This? This is just fancy."

Lily chuckled softly, her nerves easing slightly as they moved further into the room.

A familiar figure caught their attention—a tall man with sandy hair and a well-tailored suit. Daniel, the keen-eyed journalist who had assisted them in decoding old Society files, nodded at them before disappearing into the crowd.

"There's Iris," Chloe said, nodding toward a statuesque woman with piercing eyes. The private investigator, known for her talent for uncovering hidden truths, raised her glass in silent acknowledgment before vanishing behind a group of chatting diplomats.

"Everyone's here," Lily whispered. "And they seem to fit in."

"We do too," Chloe said decisively, surveying the room with sharp focus. "Just stick to the plan."

Before Lily could respond, an elegant woman in a crimson gown approached them. Her diamond necklace sparkled like a constellation, and she radiated a quiet authority that commanded attention. "Chloe and Lily, I presume?"

"Yes," Chloe replied, her tone polite yet cautious. "And who are you?"

"Eleanor Prescott," the woman said smoothly. "I'm the hostess for tonight's gala. It's a pleasure to finally meet you. Your recent endeavors have certainly caught attention."

Lily felt her stomach tighten. "Thank you for having us," she said carefully. "But … why us?"

Eleanor's lips curled into a serene smile, but her sharp eyes held a calculating glint. "People with your resourcefulness are always intriguing to my circle. Enjoy the evening, ladies. I'm sure you'll find it … enlightening." With a nod, she melted into the crowd of guests.

Chloe and Lily exchanged glances, the unspoken question hanging in the air between them.

As they continued to mingle, Chloe's gaze was drawn to a striking centerpiece in the grand foyer: a glossy black statue of an obsidian eye perched on a pedestal. Its surface caught the light in an eerie, lifelike way. Lily joined her, her eyes wide with fascination.

"That's unsettling," she whispered.

"Beautiful, isn't it?" a deep voice interjected. They turned to see an older man with silver hair and a cane. His eyes sparkled with intelligence as he observed them. "The Obsidian Eye. It's said to possess magical properties. Legends suggest it can reveal truths and expose lies."

"Magical?" Lily asked, trying to sound casual.

The man chuckled. "Stories are often exaggerated, but each one contains a kernel of truth, don't you think?" He gave a polite nod and walked away, leaving the sisters more intrigued than ever.

As the evening wore on, guarded conversations and fleeting glances filled the air. Chloe noticed Eleanor Prescott talking to a man in a military uniform. Their body language was tense, and they spoke in low voices. Meanwhile, Lily spotted a group of tech moguls whispering near the staircase, their expressions grim.

When a waiter subtly slipped a folded note into Chloe's hand, her heart raced. She pulled Lily into a quiet alcove to read it. The hastily written message was urgent yet clear: *Be careful. They know what you're doing.*

Lily's hands trembled. "What should we do now?"

"We're sticking to the plan," Chloe said, folding the note and slipping it into her clutch. "But we'll be more cautious than ever."

As the night went on, their tension increased with each passing moment. Whispers of an AI summit in Japan, climate biology initiatives in Iceland, and ancient technology research in Israel suggested a larger mystery that they were determined to unravel.

When the clock struck midnight, Chloe and Lily decided it was time to leave. They approached Eleanor, expressed their gratitude for the invitation, and stepped outside into the chilly night air. The sleek black sedan awaited them. The glow from the lavish affair dimmed as they drove away from the mansion.

In the calm of the car, the adrenaline began to fade. Lily rested her head against the window, worn out. Chloe stared into the darkness, her mind racing with fragments of conversations and the mysterious note.

"We're in over our heads," Lily murmured sleepily.

"We'll figure it out," Chloe said, her voice steady despite the heaviness in her chest. "We always do."

As the car rolled into the driveway, Lily glanced at her sister and smiled softly.

Chapter 8

Morning After

The soft glow of the morning sun filtered through the sheer curtains, casting warm strip of light across the living room. Chloe and Lily sat at the dining table, their hands wrapped around steaming mugs of coffee. The air was thick with unspoken thoughts, the tension from the gala still hanging over them like an unshakeable shadow. Neither had slept much; their minds had churned all night, fueled by the cryptic note they'd been given and the web of secrets they'd stumbled into.

Lily broke the silence, her spoon softly clinking against the mug as she stirred her coffee for what felt like the hundredth time. "I can't stop thinking about Eleanor Prescott," she said, her eyes distant. "Do you think she knows more about us than she's letting on?"

Chloe didn't hesitate. "Absolutely. Eleanor doesn't seem like the type to engage in small talk just for fun.

She invited us for a reason, and I doubt it was merely to showcase her art collection.”

Their eyes met across the table, and in that moment, their shared resolve felt as tangible as the coffee mugs in their hands. Chloe leaned back in her chair, her blonde hair still slightly tousled from a restless night. “Lily, we need help—real help. If we’re going to untangle this mess, it will take more than Gil and his friends, no matter how impressive their spy skills may be.”

Lily nodded, her fingers gliding along the rim of her mug. “What about the librarian? Mrs. Greene knows a lot about the archives, and she’s already helped us once. Maybe she has more connections.”

Chloe’s face brightened. “That’s exactly what I was thinking. If anyone knows the history of The Society— or has encountered them before—it’s her.”

After a quick breakfast and changing into their usual casual yet ready-for-anything outfits, the sisters drove to the library. The small brick building, with ivy climbing up one side, felt like an oasis of calm amid the storm they were navigating. Inside, Mrs. Greene welcomed them with her signature warm smile, sparkling with curiosity as she noticed their determined expressions.

"Chloe, Lily," she said, her voice a mix of surprise and concern. "Back so soon? What's on your minds?"

Chloe leaned against the counter, her gaze fixed on the librarian. "We were at the gala last night."

Mrs. Greene raised her eyebrows, her smile fading slightly. "Oh? What happened?"

Lily let out a dry laugh. "More … eventful than we anticipated." She glanced around to ensure no one else was within earshot. "We overheard things—and witnessed things—that made us realize The Society is more connected than we thought. We need to find people who know more, who've encountered them before. Mrs. Greene, you've already been a tremendous help, but do you know anyone else who might be willing to talk to us?"

The librarian's kind face became serious as her fingers tapped lightly on the counter. "There were a few," she said slowly. "Back when I was younger, some people poked their noses where they didn't belong. Most of them vanished, but I'll see what I can recall."

Lily's face brightened with appreciation. "Thank you very much. We can't accomplish this by ourselves."

Mrs. Greene nodded, her expression softening but still marked by concern. "Be careful, girls. The Society doesn't welcome questions. And you two remind me of your grandmother—stubborn, brave, and too clever for your own good."

The mention of their grandmother brought a brief smile to their faces. Her legacy served as the foundation of their determination, a reminder that courage ran deep within them.

As they left the library, Chloe's phone buzzed with a message from Gil: *Let's meet. I have something you need to see.*

Lily raised an eyebrow as Chloe displayed the screen. "What now?" she asked with mock exasperation, although a hint of humor flickered in her tone.

"Whatever it is, I'm sure it will only contribute to our ever-growing list of problems," Chloe said with a smirk.

But when they got home, the atmosphere inside felt … off. Chloe was the first to notice the signs: the living room window was slightly ajar, even though they had closed it before leaving, a faint scuff mark on the floor near the bookshelf, and Lily's favorite mug had been moved from the counter to the sink.

Chloe's heart raced as a chill swept down her spine. "Someone has been here," she whispered.

Lily froze in her tracks. "Are you certain?"

Chloe nodded, her eyes scanning the room. "Something feels off. Come on, we need to think smart about this." She led Lily to the bathroom and turned on the shower, the rush of water drowning out their voices. "If they've been here, they could have planted bugs."

Lily's eyes grew wide. "What should we do?"

"I'm calling Gil," Chloe said with determination. "Don't move."

Chloe walked into the backyard, phone clutched tightly in her hand, her pulse quickening. She dialled Gil's number, and each ring felt like an eternity. When his familiar voice finally came through, Chloe's relief was palpable.

"Gil," she started urgently, her voice edged with tension, "someone's been inside our house. Things have been moved—I think they may have planted bugs. It feels … invasive, calculated."

"Stay where you are," Gil replied after a brief pause. "Raj and I are on our way. Don't touch anything else."

Chloe paused. "You said you had something to show us?"

A pause. "It's huge," Gil said. "I'll explain everything once we get there."

When Gil and Raj arrived, their usual playful banter had disappeared, replaced by a mood of grim determination. Gil carried a sleek black case that looked as if it came straight out of a spy movie, while Raj rolled up his sleeves to reveal faint scars crisscrossing his forearms, hinting at a rebellious past.

"Let's sweep the house," Gil said, his tone all business.

As the two men started their careful search, Chloe and Lily stayed close, exchanging anxious looks.

Lily attempted to lighten the mood. "At least if they find a bug, we'll know The Society is taking us seriously?"

Chloe let out a dry laugh. "How comforting."

Chapter 9

Bugs and Discovery

The air in the house felt prickly with the weight of suspicion. Gil and Raj moved silently, their focus razor-sharp as they systematically scanned each room with their devices. Chloe and Lily followed closely, like anxious shadows, their nerves tense with every muted beep from the equipment.

"Okay, seriously, what are we looking for?" Chloe asked, her effort to keep her voice steady, failing miserably.

Gil kept his gaze lowered, his dark eyes fixed on the blinking device in his hand. "Bugs, cameras, anything that doesn't belong."

"Bugs? Are you talking about the crawling kind or the creepy surveillance kind?" Lily whispered, wrapping her arms around herself.

Raj stepped out of the study, holding a small black device between his thumb and forefinger. "Creepy surveillance type," he said grimly.

Lily instinctively recoiled. "That's worse than spiders. At least spiders don't *take orders* from you."

"That depends on the spider," Raj muttered with a wry smile, prompting a nervous giggle from Lily.

The search continued, each discovery increasing the sisters' anxiety. One bug had been hidden in the living room light fixture, and another stashed away in the base of a study lamp. Every time Gil removed one, Lily flinched as if it might explode.

When the house was finally declared clean, Chloe and Lily collapsed onto the couch, looking as if they had just run a marathon.

Gil placed the collected devices into a small black pouch. "We'll analyze these later, but first, we need to talk."

Raj leaned against the doorframe, his serious expression softening a bit. "You're not safe here. Whoever planted these wasn't just spying—they were sending a message."

Chloe straightened, her jaw clenched. "Well, message received. But we're not backing down. They can't scare us off."

Gil's lips twitched, almost forming a smile. "Good. You'll need that backbone for what lies ahead."

He opened his laptop, its screen casting a cold blue glow across the dim room. The screen displayed folders with cryptic labels, and Chloe observed as Lily leaned in, her curiosity overcoming her apprehension.

"This," Gil said, cycling through a series of images and diagrams, "is what we're up against. The Society isn't merely a local club of power-hungry elites; they're part of a global network involved in everything."

He displayed a photo of a vast, advanced facility set among snow-covered mountains. "This is Iceland. They're financing geoengineering experiments here—trying to manipulate global weather patterns. Imagine having the power to create a drought or a hurricane at will."

Raj tapped the screen, unveiling an image of a cutting-edge Japanese lab. "And here? Advanced AI development. We're not talking about helpful robots. We're discussing surveillance systems so invasive that they make your phone's location tracking look like child's play."

"Japan gets robots?" Lily asked, her voice trembling with nervous laughter. "We just got bugs."

Gil ignored her and pressed on. "In India, they support medical research—risky business. Custom viruses and antidotes. Imagine selling immunity to the highest bidder while keeping the cure hidden."

Chloe felt her stomach twist. "That's … gross."

Gil nodded solemnly. "And in Israel, they are developing quantum encryption. They're creating communication systems that no one can hack. If they perfect it, they'll be invulnerable. There's something else going on there too, something to do with ancient artifacts. We suspect they hold a secret to another means of control of some kind."

Lily looked pale, her hazel eyes wide. "How can we fight something like this? It's— it's like trying to punch a tornado."

Gil leaned forward, his gaze intense. "We expose them—every operation, every secret they've buried; we bring it to light. And we stop them, however we can. But you need to understand that there's no turning back once we start. They'll come for us, and they won't fight fair."

Chloe glanced at Lily. For a moment, her sister appeared impossibly young, fear clearly visible on her face. Then Lily gave a sharp nod, her expression hardening.

"We're in," Chloe declared with determination. "We've come too far to turn back now."

Raj smiled faintly. "You have courage. You'll need it."

The weight of their decision filled the room. For a brief moment, the sisters felt the magnitude of what they had just agreed to. Then Gil broke the silence with his signature dry humor.

"For now, you need a safer place to stay, ideally one without eavesdropping lamps."

Chloe offered a faint smile. "We'll find a way. But thanks, Gil. For … everything."

Gil shrugged, a faint smile tugging at the corner of his mouth. "Don't thank me just yet. The hard part is only beginning."

As the team packed their gear, Chloe and Lily glanced at each other. Despite their fear, they felt a strange sense of calm. They were no longer alone. With Gil, Raj, and their new allies, they had a real chance.

Outside, the atmosphere was quiet, with the world seemingly unaware of the battle lines being drawn within. Chloe tightened her grip on the edge of the couch, a glimmer of determination in her eyes.

"The Society has no idea what they've started," she murmured to herself.

Lily smiled. "Let's ensure they discover it."

Chapter 10

The Gathering

The heavy wooden door creaked open, its hinges protesting as if hesitant to unveil the secrets concealed beyond. A cool, earthy draft swept over Chloe, Lily, Raj, and Gil as they peered into the narrow, dimly lit tunnel beneath Upland High School's gymnasium.

"Am I the only one wondering how we ended up in a Scooby-Doo episode?" Chloe whispered, glancing at her younger sister.

Lily smirked, though her eyes darted nervously toward the shadows. "If I hear any creepy laughter, I'm out."

Mrs. Greene, the unassuming librarian who had somehow become their mentor in all things mysterious, gestured for them to follow. "Come on, girls. We don't have all night." Her voice carried a hint of amusement, but the flicker of concern in her expression unveiled the seriousness of their situation.

Behind them, Gil adjusted the strap of his laptop bag, his dark eyes scanning their surroundings like a hawk. "Well, this is cozy," he muttered, his Israeli accent adding a layer of sarcasm.

"Cozy if you like damp, creepy tunnels," Raj said, rubbing his arms as the group went deeper. "I'm just saying—can we meet at a coffee shop next time? Somewhere with Wi-Fi?"

"Somewhere without centuries-old secrets?" Chloe quipped, trying to lighten the mood, even as the cold stone walls felt like they were closing in.

The air was thick with the scent of earth and damp stone, steeped in years of history. Mrs. Greene led the way with steady confidence, pausing only to point out faintly glowing markers on the walls that seemed to guide their path.

"This tunnel was built during Prohibition," she explained, her voice echoing softly. "It has served many purposes since then—some noble and others less so. Only a few of us know it still exists."

"Let me take a guess," Lily said, stepping around a puddle. "The Society is aware of this too?"

Mrs. Greene didn't respond, but the silence spoke volumes.

After what felt like an eternity, the tunnel opened into a spacious underground chamber beneath the Madonna of the Trail statue at the intersection of Euclid and Foothill. The sight stopped them all in their tracks.

"Whoa," Lily breathed, eyes wide.

The room was breathtaking. At its center stood a massive circular table carved from a single slab of polished stone. The walls were lined with shelves brimming with ancient books, weathered artifacts, and yellowed maps. Golden lights set in the arched ceiling cast a warm, almost magical glow. A mural spanned the far wall, illustrating Upland's history, with the Madonna of the Trail standing sentinel over it all.

"This place feels like it's right out of a movie," Chloe whispered, half-expecting Indiana Jones to leap out from behind the shelves.

Mrs. Greene smiled faintly. "This has served as a sanctuary for decades—a refuge for those seeking the truth and protection from those who would try to silence it."

The group approached the table where a gathering of older Uplanders sat waiting. Each exuded an air of quiet authority, their faces marked by the lines of hard-won wisdom. One of them, a wiry man with sharp features and piercing gray eyes, stood as they entered.

"My name is Arthur Wren," he said, his voice steady but resolute. He held a leather satchel that seemed to have experienced more adventures than most people. "I've dedicated my life to uncovering the histories of artifacts—and the secrets they contain. Tonight, Mrs. Greene asked me to speak about one in particular: the Obsidian Eye."

When the artifact was mentioned, Chloe and Lily glanced at each other, and the room appeared to hold its breath.

Arthur reached into his satchel and pulled out a worn journal. "The Obsidian Eye isn't just a relic; it's a tool of immense power, believed to have been crafted in ancient Mesopotamia. It's said to reveal truths hidden from mortal eyes and to protect its bearer from deception."

"Sounds useful," Gil said as he leaned against the table. "But what's the catch?"

Arthur's eyes narrowed. "Its power comes at a price. Those who seek to wield it often become targets of those who covet its capabilities. The Society has pursued the Eye for centuries—not just to control it, but to dominate through it."

Lily shifted uncomfortably. "At the gala, we saw a statue of the Eye. Was that—?"

"A decoy," one of the others at the table interjected, nodding grimly. "But the real Eye was present too, hiding in plain sight. The Society thrives on arrogance; they flaunt their power because they believe no one can challenge them."

Chloe's heart raced. "If they already have it, what does that mean for us?"

"It means you're in danger," Arthur said bluntly. "If they even suspect that you're trying to stop them, they won't hesitate to eliminate you."

The weight of his words hung heavily in the room.

"Cool," Raj replied faintly. "No pressure."

Mrs. Greene placed a reassuring hand on Chloe's shoulder. "That's why we're here. The Society may possess the Eye, but they're not invincible. We need to understand their plans and disrupt them before they solidify their power."

Arthur unfolded a map on the table, indicating several marked locations. "These tunnels are part of a larger network that connects key sites used by The Society for centuries. If we can navigate through them, we might uncover where they've hidden the Eye."

Gil leaned forward, narrowing his eyes. "And then what? Steal it back?"

Arthur smiled slightly. "Let's find it first. Then we'll decide how to take it."

The rest of the night was spent poring over maps, sharing stories, and making plans. The other older members of the gathering offered advice and their hard-earned experience to the mix. Chloe and Lily absorbed every detail, their fear eased by a growing sense of determination.

As they emerged much later from the tunnel into the cool night air, the sisters felt a renewed sense of purpose.

"This is bigger than we realized," Lily said softly.

Chloe nodded. "Yeah, but we're not alone anymore."

For the first time in weeks, she allowed herself to hope. The battle against the Society was far from over, but they now had allies—and they wouldn't rest until the truth was uncovered.

Chapter 11

Exploring the Tunnels

As the first rays of sunlight streaked across the sky, Chloe, Lily, and the whole team gathered at the hidden tunnel entrance near Upland High School's gymnasium. Above them, the city buzzed with excitement, signaling the beginning of the annual scavenger hunt and a weekend full of celebrations. It was the perfect distraction.

"Best cover we've ever had," Gil said, tightening the straps on his old leather backpack. His dark eyes sparkled with amusement. "The streets will be crowded, and no one will notice us sneaking around beneath their feet."

Mrs. Greene, ever the practical one, handed Lily a small flashlight. "Stick together, stay quiet, and for goodness' sake, don't touch anything unless it's necessary. These tunnels are a labyrinth. Getting lost is not part of the plan."

Chloe glanced at her sister knowingly as they descended into the shadowy depths. The air grew cooler, and the city's noise faded into an eerie silence. The walls, hewed from stone, whispered secrets of the past. Etched symbols and weathered carvings hinted at stories that time had long buried.

"Creepy, but sort of cool," Lily whispered, her eyes darting around. She traced a faint mark on the wall with her finger. "I wonder how old this is."

Mrs. Greene stopped suddenly, brushing dust off a small emblem. "This is the symbol of the Chaffey brothers," she said softly. "They built the irrigation systems that enabled this region to thrive. But The Society … they distorted their efforts, using these very tunnels to hide their secrets."

Lily frowned. "Is there any part of Upland *that isn't* intertwined with The Society?"

Chloe pressed her lips into a thin line. "I'm skeptical. But it gives us more places to look for answers."

The group ventured deeper into the tunnels, passing relics of bygone eras—a crumbling wine cellar from Prohibition, shelves lined with dust-covered jars, and faded ledgers bearing the name *The Olive House*. Arthur Wren, the artifact expert, could hardly contain his excitement.

"Check this out!" he exclaimed, raising a rusty wrench. "Tools like this were crucial to Upland's early industries. The Olive House alone revolutionized olive oil production in the area."

"Focus, Arthur," Chloe said with a smirk. "We're not here to build a museum."

As they came upon a fork in the tunnel, a wave of tension washed over the group. One path emitted a faint glow, while the other opened into a dark void.

"The light leads to an exit near the Magic Lamp Restaurant," Mrs. Greene explained, her fingers tracing the wall. "It's seldom used. But the darker path …" She hesitated. "Old maps suggest it leads to a hidden chamber."

Chloe narrowed her eyes. "We didn't come this far to choose the easy path. We're going dark."

Gil chuckled. "That's a saying straight from a genuine adventurer."

The team pressed on, their flashlights casting long, flickering shadows. The walls closed in slightly, and the air became damp and cold. The silence felt oppressive, broken only by the soft crunch of their footsteps.

Finally, they discovered it: a set of iron doors, partly buried in debris.

Arthur's excitement reignited as he crouched down to inspect the intricate carvings on the metal. "Protective runes," he whispered. "The creator of this sought to conceal something—or keep *us* away."

Gil pulled on the handle with force. Nothing. "Of course, it's locked."

Lily stepped forward, pulling a sleek case from her jacket pocket. "Step aside, gentlemen. Grandma taught me a few tricks." Her fingers glided over the lock with practiced ease.

"You can pick locks?" Raj asked, raising his eyebrows.

Lily smiled. "I'm a woman of many talents."

With a satisfying click, the doors creaked open, revealing a vast chamber. Beams of their flashlights pierced the gloom, illuminating a pedestal in the center. Atop it sat a small, locked chest, its metal surface darkened with age.

"This is a trap," Raj muttered, maintaining his distance.

Chloe approached carefully, her muscles tense. "Maybe. But we're here for answers."

Arthur's voice trembled with excitement. "These markings … they match descriptions of artifacts connected to The Society." He gestured toward the chest. "This could be a breakthrough."

Gil carefully unlatched the chest, moving purposefully. Inside, he discovered a set of documents, a map, and a small black orb that softly shimmered in the dim light.

"Is this … the Obsidian Eye?" Lily asked, her voice filled with awe.

Arthur shook his head. "No. But this could be a fragment of it, a piece reconfigured—a conduit that might help locate or harness the Eye's power."

Chloe opened the map, her heart racing. Red circles marked locations scattered throughout Upland—and beyond. "Here, look, Mt. Baldy and The Olive House are circled. Both could be significant."

"Mt. Baldy makes sense," Gil said. "It's remote, defensible, and perfect for hiding something important. The Olive House, though …"

Mrs. Greene nodded. "It's now a historic site—perfect for concealing their activities."

Chloe carefully folded the map. "Let's secure this fragment. Then at some point we can split up. Some of us need to go to Mt. Baldy, while the others head to The Olive House. The Society is planning something, and we've got to stop it."

As they wound their way back through the tunnels, the significance of their discovery whirled in their minds. The stakes had never been higher. Humor and banter couldn't hide the tension, but it strengthened their resolve. They were a team now—unlikely allies brought together by fate and a shared mission.

Chapter 12

Tracking Down the Eye

The dim glow in the hidden chamber beneath the Madonna of the Trail statue cast long, flickering shadows across the ancient walls. Chloe and Lily leaned over the newly discovered map, their fingers tracing the delicate, intricate lines and mysterious symbols. Each mark seemed to exhale secrets long buried.

"This place gives me the creeps," Lily muttered, glancing around the room. Her eyes scanned every corner as if she expected a ghost—or worse, a member of The Society—to appear.

"You're not wrong," Chloe replied, her eyes sharp with focus. "But take a look at this." She tapped a spot on the map, her voice low and urgent. "An old estate on the outskirts of Upland. The notes indicate it has been abandoned for decades. It appears to have been owned by the Hawthornes."

Gil leaned over her shoulder, his warm breath brushing against a strand of Chloe's hair. "That symbol," he murmured, his deep voice filled with concern, "is not a coincidence. The Society won't wait for us to figure this out. If they're ahead of us, we're in serious trouble."

"And we're not really behind them, are we?" Luca smirked, spinning a USB drive between his fingers like a magician's wand. "With me tracking their digital moves, they won't get far."

"Unless they're using analog tricks," Yuki said dryly, adjusting the strap of her tactical vest. "I'll take point. No offense, but most of you wouldn't last ten seconds in a booby-trapped building."

"No offense taken," Lily quipped, raising her hands in a playful gesture of surrender. "I'm better at fleeing from danger than charging into it."

Thalia, standing near the entrance, finally spoke up. Her voice was calm yet held a quiet intensity. "You'll need more than technology and courage to decipher the symbols on that map. These markings are linked to ancient lore—things The Society has likely studied for decades. Let me help. I've encountered similar patterns in my research."

The group turned to look at her, their expressions a blend of curiosity and surprise. Chloe nodded slowly. "If you have any insight into this, we'll need it."

"I don't merely have insight," Thalia said, stepping closer. "I've studied The Society's ancient texts. This map isn't just a clue—it's a warning."

The Ruins of the Hawthorne Estate

The estate stood like a lost nightmare, its once-grand façade overtaken by a tangle of ivy and decay. Broken windows gazed like hollow eyes, and the scent of damp earth and mildew hung in the air.

"This place should come with a haunted warning," Lily whispered, sticking close to Chloe as they crossed the crumbling threshold. Their flashlights sliced narrow beams of light through the darkness, revealing faded wallpaper that peeled like old skin and furniture cloaked in dust thicker than snow.

"Stay alert," Yuki commanded, her voice almost a whisper. "Anything unusual could be a clue—or a trap."

Thalia moved to the front of the group, her sharp eyes scanning the room. She suddenly stopped, crouching near an ornate, cracked mirror. "Here," she said, brushing away dust to reveal faint etchings in the glass. "This is part of the same code as on the map. It's a sequence—like a puzzle."

Chloe knelt beside her. "What kind of puzzle?"

"It's meant to test you," Thalia replied. "The Society uses these codes to weed out anyone who doesn't have the knowledge—and the courage—to move forward."

In what appeared to be a study, Chloe's flashlight illuminated a faint carving etched into a wooden bookshelf. She ran her fingers over the grooves, her heart racing. "Lily, come here."

Lily crouched beside her. "It's the same symbol as on the map, but it seems … incomplete."

Yuki examined it, her sharp eyes narrowing. "It's a device. Step back. Let me give it a try."

With a soft click, Yuki activated the hidden mechanism. The bookshelf creaked open, revealing a narrow passageway. Cold air rushed out, carrying the faint metallic scent of something ancient.

At the end of the passage, a pedestal gleamed in their flashlight beams. Atop it rested an ornate compass, its needle spinning lazily as if waiting for direction. Beside it lay a parchment covered in faded writing.

"This isn't just a compass," Arthur whispered, his voice filled with wonder. "It's attuned to energy. If the Obsidian Eye is real, this will lead us to it."

Thalia studied the parchment intently, her expression unreadable. "This writing is a riddle," she said softly. "It's in an ancient dialect, but I can translate. It refers to aligning the compass with the peaks of Mt. Baldy."

"That means the Society might already be on their way there," Einar said grimly, clenching his fists. "We're in a race."

A Rift Among Allies

In the underground chamber, the air was thick with tension as Chloe and Lily revealed their discovery. The rest of the team listened intently, but unease hovered just below the surface.

"This compass could be our breakthrough," Chloe said. "But we must hurry."

Raj stood at the edge of the group with his arms crossed. "What if it's a trap? What if The Society placed that compass to lure us out?"

Chloe glanced at him sharply. "Yes, it's a risk, but this whole mission is full if risk, isn't it? Can we afford to ignore what this could mean for us?"

Raj shook his head. "I still think it's not a good idea to go haring off on a guess."

Gil clenched his jaw. "Well it's a risk we've thought about. But we can't let fear hold us back."

Thalia stepped forward, her voice calm but firm. "Raj has a point. But so does Gil. The Society is ruthless, but they don't expect us to outthink them. That's our advantage." She turned to Chloe. "I'll work on decoding more of the riddle while you plan the next move."

Chloe nodded. "We'll need everything you've got."

Glancing again at Raj she felt uneasy. Why was he suddenly so seemingly careful?

Betrayal Confirmed

The next morning at the safe house, Chloe's intuition was confirmed. Raj and his gear were missing. His phone, abandoned in a rush, held a series of encrypted messages. Luca decoded them with a grim expression.

"He's been passing intel to The Society," Luca announced. "They're now aware of the compass, the riddle—everything."

Aoife pounded her fist on the table, her face clouded with anger. "I trusted him. We all did."

"Trust is a double-edged sword," Yuki said coolly, though a glimmer of pain shone in her eyes. "But we can't dwell on it. We need to take action."

Chloe's hands shook as she gripped the compass. "Raj betrayed us, but he won't stop us. We're headed to Mt. Baldy, and we will put an end to this."

Thalia gently placed a reassuring hand on Chloe's shoulder. "We'll figure this out, and we'll ensure The Society doesn't win."

The team packed their gear in a grim, determined silence. The race for the Obsidian Eye had truly begun.

Chapter 13

Crossroads of Trust

The underground chamber hummed with tension. Lantern light flickered on the ancient stone walls, illuminating the scattered maps, notes, and diagrams laid out across the table. Chloe stood with her arms crossed, her face fixed in a determined expression.

Thalia leaned against a pillar with her arms crossed. "Raj isn't wasting any time, and we shouldn't either. What's the plan?"

Gil, standing at the head of the table, let out a sharp exhale. "The compass and the riddle point to Mt. Baldy, but The Society may already be ahead of us. We need to act quickly—and carefully."

Arthur, seated at a nearby desk, adjusted his reading glasses while examining the parchment. "I'd go with you if I could," he said, his voice filled with regret, "but my knees wouldn't handle that steep climb. Take photos of anything important. I'll be here to help interpret whatever you find. We can stay in touch on the phone. Keep a line open so I can hear what's unfolding. I'll text in case you need silent communication."

"We'll make sure to document everything," Chloe assured him.

Aoife, standing by the table with her hands on her hips, examined the markings on the parchment. "This map doesn't just show directions," she said, her Irish lilt adding a contemplative rhythm. "It's also a geospatial alignment guide. Whoever created this used natural energy lines in the mountains to conceal something significant."

Arthur looked up, intrigued. "You've worked with energy line theories before, haven't you?"

Aoife nodded. "As a geospatial analyst, I've encountered maps like this. They're not only about pinpointing the right location—they're also concerned with timing. If the compass isn't properly aligned with the energy points on this map, we could completely overlook what it's indicating."

Einar, who had been quietly observing, stepped forward. His broad frame seemed to fill the room, yet his voice was calm and steady. "Aoife's right. These markings correspond with fault lines and geothermal activity. If we're dealing with something buried underground, we need to consider how the terrain shifts. The mountain itself may be working against us."

Chloe turned to Einar, her eyes narrowing thoughtfully. "You've studied fault lines extensively, haven't you?"

He nodded. "Years of monitoring seismic activity; if The Society has been working in this area, they've likely exploited the natural instability to conceal their efforts. However, it also indicates they may have triggered shifts that we will need to navigate."

Climbing up Mt. Baldy

Morning broke crisp and cold, with Mt. Baldy's jagged peaks shrouded in wisps of mist. The group assembled at the trailhead, their breath visible in the frigid air. Chloe adjusted her pack, feeling the weight of their mission pressing down as heavily as her supplies.

"Thalia, Yuki, take the lead," Gil instructed. "Mei, have the compass ready. Luca, make sure Arthur stays connected—no technical issues."

Aoife stepped up, securing her gear. "I'll chart the energy points along the way and ensure we don't veer off

course. The terrain can change unexpectedly."

Einar tossed his pack over his shoulder, his expression inscrutable. "I'll monitor the fault lines. If we come across any unstable areas, I'll ensure we're not caught off guard."

The trail began gently, winding through tall pine trees. Sunlight filtered through the branches, casting patterns on the forest floor, and the air was filled with the rich aroma of earth and resin. As they climbed, the incline steepened, displacing loose rocks underfoot, and their breathing became more labored.

"This is fun," Luca grumbled, wiping the sweat from his forehead. "I can't think of a better way to spend my morning than hauling myself up a glorified pile of dirt and rocks."

"You'd find a way to complain about winning the lottery," Thalia quipped, glancing back at him with a smirk.

Einar let out a soft chuckle. "You'd complain about the weight of the money."

The group laughed, their spirits lifting slightly.

An hour into the climb, Mei stopped abruptly. "Here," she said, pointing to a jagged boulder marked with faint carvings. These match the markings on the parchment."

Aoife crouched down to examine the boulder. "This isn't just a waypoint marker—it's part of a larger alignment system. The ridgeline there"—she pointed to a nearby peak—"connects directly to the next point on the map. If we veer off course, we could miss what we're searching for."

Einar examined the rocky terrain surrounding the marker, his brow furrowing. "This area is prone to small shifts. A recent tremor could have disrupted the alignment. If we're off by even a few degrees, we might miss the entrance."

Chloe nodded. "Let's stay on track. Keep the compass aligned with the map."

The Hidden Alcove

By late afternoon, the group reached a secluded alcove near the summit. The air was thinner, and the mist clung to the ground like a living being. At the center of the area stood a stone pillar, its carvings more intricate than anything they had seen before.

Mei lifted the compass, its needle spinning erratically and softly glowing. "This has to be it."

Aoife crouched near the base of the pillar, running her hands along the grooves. "This isn't just decorative; these carvings align with the mountain's energy lines." She pulled out her journal, flipping to a sketch she had made earlier. "If the compass isn't aligned perfectly with these grooves, the mechanism won't activate properly."

Einar knelt beside her, his large hands steady as he traced the grooves. "There's fresh damage here—probably from a tremor. It's minor, but if we don't adjust the alignment, the mechanism could jam or cause a collapse."

Thalia quickly snapped a series of pictures and sent them to Arthur. Chloe checked her phone when his response arrived: *These inscriptions caution about balance and sacrifice. Align the compass with the lens and let the sunlight guide you. But be careful—such mechanisms often contain traps.* She quickly read it out.

As they worked together, Aoife guided Mei in adjusting the compass while Einar stabilized the grooves to ensure smooth alignment.

"Careful now," Aoife warned. "The grooves here are fragile. If we're off by even a degree, we could trigger something we can't undo."

As sunlight filtered through the mist, it hit the lens, creating a beam of light that revealed a hidden engraving on the distant wall.

"It's a map," Luca said as he took a picture. "And it appears to indicate an underground network beneath the mountain."

"I'm sending it to Arthur now," Thalia said, typing quickly.

Trouble

Before they could celebrate, Yuki stopped, raising a hand for silence. "We're not alone," she whispered.

The sound of boots crunching on gravel echoed through the alcove. Shadows shifted in the light mist and they could make out Raj advancing, flanked by a number of men in black.

Chapter 14

Into the Depths

The air atop Mt. Baldy was sharp, the crisp chill biting at Chloe's cheeks as she scanned the ridgeline. Shadows stretched longer through the mist in the amber glow of the setting sun. Behind her, the group shifted uneasily, their breath fogging in the cold.

Chloe gripped the strap of her bag, her voice just above a whisper. "Yuki, can we avoid a fight?"

Yuki shook her head, her sharp gaze fixed on the approaching silhouettes. "No. They've boxed us in. Running isn't an option."

Gil adjusted his makeshift walking stick, the leather of his jacket creaking softly as he moved. His wry grin didn't quite reach his eyes. "Then let's make it a fight they'll remember."

Einar stepped to the front of the group, his imposing frame serving as a shield of strength and composure.

"Stay behind me," he said in his deep, steady voice. "No one's getting through unless they face me first."

Aoife stepped forward, her expression calm yet calculating. "They won't pass. But if Raj is here, he isn't just after us. He's after whatever's concealed in these mountains. There's more at stake than just a fight."

Chloe nodded, trusting Aoife's instincts. "Then we outsmart him."

Raj stepped into the clearing, his smug expression accentuated by the fading light. His men spread out behind him, their weapons glimmering. "You're out of your league," he shouted. "The Society isn't something you can conquer. Hand over the compass and the map, and maybe—just maybe—you'll manage to walk away."

Chloe stepped forward, her chin held high and her voice clear and defiant. "You betrayed us, Raj. You don't get to make deals anymore."

Raj briefly hesitated, his smile fading before he regained his composure. His voice was steeped in threat. "I admire your courage, Chloe, but bravery won't protect you from the fate that awaits those who oppose The Society."

Runes on the Pillar

Mei ran her hands over a carved stone pillar nearby, her brow furrowed in concentration. "This pillar—it's a mechanism. If I can activate it, we could discover an escape route underground," she whispered urgently.

Thalia stood beside her, tracing her fingers along the ancient carvings. Her voice was low, calm yet assertive. "These aren't just any carvings. They're wayfinders—symbols used to align hidden pathways. This isn't simply an escape route. It's a direct connection to whatever the map leads us to."

Mei glanced at Thalia, impressed. "You've seen these before?"

"In fragments," Thalia answered, her dark eyes examining the intricate lines. "But never anything this detailed, intact. If we activate this, we're going exactly where The Society wants us to go—but faster."

Chloe didn't hesitate. "Do it."

While Thalia and Mei worked to activate the pillar, Yuki and Einar took up defensive positions with deliberate and practiced movements. When Raj's men surged forward, the group fought back with everything they had. Yuki's precision disarmed one attacker in seconds, her movements fluid and controlled. Einar held off two men simultaneously, his sheer strength overpowering their efforts.

"Got it!" Mei shouted as the pillar came to life. The ground beneath them quaked, and a section of earth shifted to reveal a dark, gaping tunnel.

"Let's move, get inside! Now!" Gil commanded.

The group rushed into the passage as Raj shouted orders that echoed behind them. Gil was the last to descend, pulling a lever just inside the entrance. The grinding of stone reverberated through the chamber, sealing them in darkness.

The Underground Network

The passage was tight and strangely humid. Their flashlights created flickering beams on walls marked by faint carvings. The air was thick with the aroma of moss and earth, and the sound of their footsteps echoed hauntingly.

"What is this place?" Lily whispered, her voice filled with wonder.

Thalia crouched next to a series of carvings, tracing her fingers along the grooves. "It's a crossroads," she murmured. "This network wasn't just designed to hide people—it's a guide to something important."

Aoife, crouching nearby, wrote notes in her journal. "The symbols are protective; they were designed to keep something—or someone—hidden from the outside world."

Chloe glanced at Thalia. "Can you read them?"

Thalia nodded. "I can interpret some of it, but these inscriptions are older than anything I've studied. We'll need to take photos and cross-reference them with Arthur's library when we get back."

"We'll figure this out," Yuki said firmly. "Stay alert. If Raj's men find another way in, we won't have much warning."

A Pivotal Puzzle

The group pressed forward, navigating obstacles that felt like they had been lifted from an ancient adventure tale. In one chamber, they encountered a puzzle: a wall of rotating stone discs engraved with cryptic symbols.

"This is no ordinary lock," Thalia said, studying the discs. "It's a star map, crafted to align with specific constellations."

"Which constellations?" Mei asked, her brow furrowing as she studied the symbols.

Thalia smiled, a rare moment of self-confidence breaking through her usual composure. "If we can align the discs with Orion's Belt, it should activate the mechanism."

The group quickly surrounded the stone discs, their flashlights casting flickering shadows across the symbols etched into the stone. Mei moved her fingers meticulously across the carvings, whispering softly to herself as she decoded the mechanical intricacies.

"These three discs represent Orion's primary stars—Alnitak, Alnilam, Mintaka," Thalia guided calmly. "Align each with the corresponding celestial marker on the wall behind."

"Got it," Mei nodded, her nimble fingers rotating each disc carefully. She paused briefly, recalibrating her approach as one disc momentarily jammed, then exhaled slowly, overcoming her hesitation and pushing gently until it clicked smoothly into place.

Around them, the tension grew palpable; each passing second amplified by the faint echo of approaching pursuit. Gil and Yuki maintained an anxious guard, eyes scanning the darkness. Einar stood close, monitoring faint tremors beneath their feet, his face alert.

"Almost there," Mei murmured, aligning the final disc. At last, the discs locked into position, and a gently glowing path emerged ahead.

"Orion's Belt," Thalia whispered. "A guide through the darkness."

A New Discovery

They stepped into a vast chamber, its walls adorned with swirling inscriptions that seemed to shimmer beneath their flashlight beams. In the center of the room stood a pedestal holding a small, softly glowing obsidian orb.

"This isn't just a fragment," Thalia said, her voice filled with reverence. "It's definitely another conduit—an amplifier for the power contained in the Eye."

Chloe took several pictures of the chamber and the orb. "Arthur needs to see this."

Arthur's response finally came through. *Again, this isn't the Eye, but it's critical—likely another part of it. Watch out for traps; the Society won't make this easy.*

Lily gazed at the orb, her voice shaking with awe. "If this is merely a fragment, what could the real Eye do?"

"We don't want to find out," Yuki replied, her tone sharp.

Defend!

A distant rumble shattered the stillness, and the ground beneath their feet trembled. Dust drifted from the ceiling, and the orb flickered ominously.

"They're in the tunnels," Luca said grimly, as his device detected movement.

"The Society," Yuki muttered darkly. "They're coming."

Chloe clutched the strap of her bag, her voice firm. "We maintain this position. Protect the fragment and the knowledge. No matter what."

Chapter 15

Betrayal and a New Ally

The underground chamber throbbed with tension. The air grew heavier with each pulse of the obsidian fragment's faint glow, its rhythm unsettling—like a heartbeat just out of sync. Chloe paced near the center of the room, phone in hand, glancing at the incoming texts from Arthur.

The glyphs could signify a map or a warning. Please send me more angles and details; we're running out of time.

"Arthur believes the symbols could signify more than mere directions," Chloe said, breaking the silence. "We must get this right."

Luca leaned against a wall, his tablet balanced in one hand. "We'll get it right," he said, typing quickly. "I'm scanning everything as a backup, just in case someone"—he shot a pointed look at Yuki—"triggers something and we have to bolt."

Yuki glanced over her shoulder, unimpressed. "You're welcome to take charge, Luca. Just make sure to avoid the booby traps."

"Relax," Luca said, smirking. "I'm not suicidal. That's your department."

"Enough," Gil snapped, her sharp tone cutting through their banter. "Focus. We're on a time limit."

Interpreting the Glyphs

Aoife knelt by the carved wall, her fingers tracing the faint symbols etched in the stone. "These markings are connected to the mountain's natural energy lines," she said, her Irish lilt reflective. "Whoever made this was using the terrain itself to conceal something."

Einar crouched beside her, studying the wall with his steady gaze. "These symbols align with fault lines. If they're connected to seismic activity, it could suggest that this entire chamber is unstable."

Gil stepped closer, his brow furrowed. "So, we're sitting in a potential earthquake zone?"

"Not just potential," Aoife corrected, pointing to a crack running along the floor. "This place has already shifted. If we're not careful, we could trigger something catastrophic."

Thalia, standing near the fragment, crossed her arms. "Then we need to quickly determine the purpose of these glyphs. The fragment's glow intensifies when it's close to certain symbols. It's reacting to the energy in this chamber."

"Arthur wants better pictures of the glyphs," Chloe said. She crouched next to Aoife, angling her phone toward the wall. "We need to ensure we capture every detail."

Luca shifted his weight, glancing between Chloe and the door. "We should also develop an exit strategy. I'm pretty sure our 'friends' aren't far behind."

The Capture

The explosion hit with the force of a thunderclap, shaking the chamber and causing debris to tumble from the ceiling. The group staggered, coughing as dust clouded the air.

"Positions!" Gil shouted, his voice cutting through the chaos. He moved swiftly, pulling Chloe and Luca behind a fallen stone pillar before taking a defensive stance near the entrance.

The chamber's sealed door had been blown open, and through the swirling haze, Raj emerged with a squad of black-clad Society agents. Their weapons gleamed ominously in the fragment's light.

"Take the fragment!" Raj ordered, his tone cold and intentional. "Leave no witnesses."

Einar charged forward with a guttural roar, swinging his makeshift weapon. His sheer size and strength made him an imposing force, but the Society agents moved with practiced precision. Gil moved in sync, using Einar's bulk as cover while delivering precise, devastating strikes to the nearest agent. His movements were fluid, a deadly dance of fists and feet.

"Aoife, Luca!" Chloe shouted, gripping the fragment. "Help Thalia secure the glyphs!"

Aoife dashed to the carvings, her journal in hand, while Luca struggled with his tablet, his fingers racing across the screen. "I'm trying to save the data before they blow us to bits!" he yelled.

Thalia remained by the fragment, her voice steady yet urgent. "Chloe, we can't allow them to take this. It's too dangerous."

"Gil, take cover on the left!" Chloe shouted as Yuki ducked beside her, taking down an incoming agent with a sweep of her leg.

"On it!" Gil turned to face another attacker, his fist slamming into the agent's jaw and sending them tumbling.

Amid the chaos, an agent grabbed Lily, yanking her away from Chloe's side.

"Lily!" Chloe screamed, starting toward her.

Raj lifted his gun, aiming it straight at Lily's head. "One more step," he threatened, "and she's finished."

The chamber fell silent. Chloe's chest rose and fell quickly as she froze, her mind racing.

"It's okay," Lily whispered, her voice trembling yet brave. "Find the Eye. Stop them."

Before anyone could react, Raj and his men disappeared into the tunnels, manhandling Lily along with them. Their footsteps echoed and faded until all that remained was the heavy silence of the chamber.

Chloe's phone buzzed, and Arthur's text appeared on the screen: *What happened?*

"They took Lily," she replied, her hands trembling.

Arthur's response came quickly: *Focus. You'll get her back. Stay alert. We're not done yet.*

Gil placed a hand on her shoulder to offer reassurance. "We'll bring her back, Chloe. I promise."

Chloe looked up, her frantic eyes meeting his. "We *have* to."

A New Ally

Before anyone could say anything else, a low voice echoed from the shadows. "Not without help, you won't."

Weapons were raised as the group turned toward the sound. A tall woman stepped into the faint light, exuding a commanding presence. Her pale skin seemed to glow in the dimness, and her piercing green eyes reflected both intelligence and a hint of pain. Jet-black hair streaked with silver framed her face, and a worn cloak draped over her shoulders, its edges tattered and frayed.

"Who are you?" Yuki asked, her posture defensive.

"Seraphine," the woman said calmly, her voice soft with a hint of a French accent. "I've been tracking The Society for years. If you want your sister back, you'll need my help."

Aoife stepped forward, her expression doubtful. "Why should we trust you?"

Seraphine met her gaze steadily. "Because I know where they're taking her, and I understand the tunnels better than they do. Or you do, for that matter."

Gil folded his arms, his tone pointed. "What's your angle?"

Seraphine's jaw tightened, yet her voice stayed steady. "The same as yours. They once took someone from me as well."

Chloe had a running open line to Arthur; he could hear everything. Arthur's message buzzed on Chloe's phone. *Who is she? Can you trust her?*

Chloe glanced at the message, her fingers swiftly dancing across the screen. *We currently have no choice.*

"If you're lying—" Gil began, his voice hard.

"You'll be the last thing I see," Seraphine interrupted, her tone sharp as steel. "But if we waste any more time, Lily might be the one who pays the price."

Going Deeper

With Seraphine leading the way, the group ventured deeper into the tunnels, their determination strengthening with each step. Chloe kept sending updates to Arthur, taking pictures of the glyphs and carvings they found.

Aoife and Thalia walked side by side, quietly discussing the carvings. "These symbols aren't just warnings," Thalia said. "They're part of a larger system—something ancient and powerful."

Aoife nodded. "The Society didn't just stumble upon this. They've been working toward it for years."

Gil walked next to Chloe, speaking softly. "We'll get Lily back."

"We just … *have* to," Chloe replied, a lump in her throat constricting here voice. She gripped the obsidian fragment tightly. Its glow appeared to pulse in sync with her determination.

The group continued, aware that their mission was far from finished.

Chapter 16

Trials and Trust

With each step, the tunnels seemed to wrap them in deeper darkness, the atmosphere pressing on them like a living presence. Their flashlights darted through the blackness, yet it felt like the very shadows were escaping from the light. In Chloe's hand, the soft glow of the obsidian fragment pulsed gently, almost comforting, like a heartbeat. She grasped it tighter, vaguely reassured, her nerves buzzing.

"I don't like this," Chloe muttered under her breath. "Are we just wandering around or looking for my sister?"

"None of us like it, Chloe, but let's give this woman a chance. We have no choice anyway." Gil replied, walking just a step behind her. His eyes scanned every corner, and his body was tense like a coiled spring.

Ahead of them, Seraphine led the way with an ease that made it clear she had walked these tunnels a hundred times before. She wasn't looking around for clues, she wasn't hesitating. She knew where she was going.

"How much further?" Chloe asked, her worry strident in her voice.

"Not much," Seraphine said without looking back. "This network of tunnels link layers—a series of chambers, stacked up on above the other. The Society's base is probably in the lowest chamber. That's where they would take her."

"Are you really sure about that?" Yuki asked skeptically. She stopped in her tracks, crossed her arms and glared at Seraphine's back. "You seem to know a whole lot about this place, but you haven't told us how you managed to appear here, now, or why. Why should we trust you?"

Gil sighed and looked at Yuki. "Let's not argue right now. If she takes us where we need to go, we can ask her questions later."

"This could be a trap, Gil." Yuki whispered.

"I know, but we're out of options." he responded.

Seraphine paused and glanced over her shoulder, her voice steady yet assertive. "You don't have to trust me, but you do need me. Unless, of course, you'd prefer to attempt navigating the Trial of Stones alone?"

"Is that supposed to scare us?" Luca quipped, though his usual grin was missing.

"It should," Seraphine said as she began to walk again. "The Trial of Stones isn't forgiving."

A nervous silence descended on the group as they contemplated what Seraphine had just said. What exactly was she leading them into?

Hearing Lily

As the group rounded a sharp corner, Chloe's heart raced when voices echoed faintly through the tunnel. She halted in her tracks, raising a hand to silence the others.

"Did you hear that?" she whispered.

"Voices," Thalia confirmed, her tone soft but alert. "They're close."

Chloe held her breath, straining to hear more clearly. The faint words became clearer—frustrated, angry tones merged with a voice she recognized all too well. Lily. Chloe's stomach churned as she caught bits of her sister's defiant replies.

"Lily," she whispered, her grip tightening around the fragment.

As they crept nearer, Raj's voice came next, cold and measured. "Tell me what your team knows about the Eye. It'll make things easier for you."

Chloe clenched her jaw. She gripped the fragment in her hand even tighter as if it amplified her anger.

Chloe heard Lily's refusal, followed by the clear sounds of a struggle. She could feel the rage rising within her and she would have raced forward blindly, if it weren't for the hand Seraphine placed on her shoulder.

"If we can hear them, then it means they are in a lower chamber after all. The tunnels carry sounds from the lower chambers upwards. This means they're close, but we can't just rush in. If they hear us coming, they won't hesitate to hurt her."

Chloe gritted her teeth, but she nodded. She knew Seraphine had a point. "Fine, then let's not give them a chance to."

Gil stepped forward, his expression serious yet calm. "Stick to the plan. We'll get her back. But no heroics, okay?"

Chloe gave him a tight smile. "No promises."

The Trial of Stones

The air became colder as the group followed Seraphine into a narrower descending passage. Under the fragment's glow, the walls glittered faintly, and intricate carvings became visible along the tunnel floor.

"Wait," Gil said, holding up a hand. He pointed to the ground. "Look."

The group froze, gazing at the glowing symbols carved into the floor. They appeared to pulse softly, as if they were alive.

"These are protective sigils," Thalia said, crouching down to examine them. "Patterns connected to mechanisms to keep artifacts safe. Step on the wrong one, and we might not escape."

"Great," Luca muttered. "Is there any chance we have an instruction manual for this?"

"It's a star map," Mei said from where she was kneeling, pointing to the carvings on the walls. "Do you see the patterns? Orion, Lyra … they're all here. If we follow the paths they create, we should be fine."

Aoife knelt beside her, flipping through her journal. "From what I can make out, the energy flow in this tunnel is connected to the arrangement of these symbols. We mustn't disrupt the sequence—we'll need to proceed carefully."

Holding her breath, Yuki tested the first step, her boot landing on one of the marked symbols. It glimmered softly but didn't react otherwise. "Looks like this one's safe … don't mess it up," she said exhaling in relief.

Mei and Aoife proceeded to set the course, consulting Aoife's journal and the star map intermittently. One by one they followed the pattern. Chloe's heart pounded as she stepped onto each sigil, her palms slick with sweat. The faint hum of the symbols seemed to grow louder with every step, the tension tightening like a rope.

As the last of them took the final step, the final sigil clicked into place and the floor shifted, revealing a larger chamber beyond.

"That was too close," Chloe said, exhaling shakily.

Gil smirked. "Come on, admit it, you love the thrill."

She rolled her eyes, but a slight smile reluctantly appeared on her face. "You wish."

Old Friend Turned Enemy

The next chamber was darker, with walls made of reflective black stone. The obsidian fragment's glow brightened the walls, creating sharp, jagged patterns.

Just then, the obsidian fragment in Chloe's hand began to flicker erratically, like an unseen force was attempting to dim it.

The team looked around, desperate to find the source of the fragment's behavior.

A figure emerged from the shadows.

"Who are you?" Seraphine asked, putting out a hand to stop the rest of the team from moving forward. Yuki froze, her eyes wide with recognition.

"Kaya?" she whispered.

The woman who stepped forward smirked, her black combat suit glinting in the fractured light. "Hello, Yuki. Surprised?"

"What are you doing here? How … wait, are you … You're part of The Society!" Yuki asked, her voice trembling with betrayal.

Kaya shrugged casually. "I've always been with them; I just didn't let you know. But I'll give you credit for getting this far. We kept this location a secret—until now. Not that it matters."

Einar stepped forward, his voice deep and rumbling. "Step aside."

Kaya's smirk grew as she pulled a blade from her belt. "Make me."

Before anyone could intervene, Kaya lunged at Yuki. Their movements blurred as the two engaged in a fierce and precise fight—years of shared training transformed into a bitter clash. The rest of the group dispersed as agents emerged from hidden alcoves.

Gil moved with deadly efficiency, disarming one agent after another. Chloe ducked behind cover, the fragment clutched tightly in her hand as she tried to make sense of the chaos. Beside her, Thalia was focusing on the carvings on the walls which had begun to glow, pulsing. The fragment was flashing.

"The fragment is responding to something! Quick, Chloe! Do you see this part of the wall that's glowing the brightest?" she said, pointing at the carvings closest to her.

"Yes," Chloe said, rushing closer.

"Shine the light from the fragment over it, let's see what happens."

Chloe did as she was told, raising the obsidian fragment up so the flashing light fell upon the carving. The walls began to shake and vibrate as a narrow passage started to reveal itself.

"A shortcut!" Seraphine yelled, rushing past Chloe into the narrow passageway that seemed to descend further. "This way!"

The Rescue

The team ran into the passageway, leaving groaning Society agents on the ground in their wake, and maneuvering the entrance closed shut behind them. They contorted their bodies to the twists and turns of this narrow corridor. At the end of it, they found Lily in the next chamber, tied up to a chair and gagged. Her face looked pale as she looked up at the people streaming into the space, but she lit up as she saw her sister.

"Chloe!" she cried, her voice breaking, as Chloe rushed to her and pulled the gag down. Chloe sliced through the ropes with shaky hands. "I've got you. You're safe now."

Lily clung to her sister, tears streaming down her face. "They're planning something big. Raj kept talking about a convergence point. They're going to—"

A tremor shook the ground, interrupting her. Dust and debris rained down from the ceiling as the group huddled closer together for protection.

"What now?" Mei exclaimed.

MADONNA OF THE TRAID
N·S·D·A·R· MEMORIAL
PIONEER MOTHERS
COVERED WAGON DAYS

Chapter 17

Shadows of the Past

The tremor rippled through the chamber, shaking loose ancient dust and debris from the cracks above. Chloe held onto Lily tightly, her heart hammering against her ribs. The ground beneath them groaned, as if the entire structure was shifting. For a terrifying second, she thought it might collapse altogether.

The others stood frozen, wide-eyed as they held onto each other. Just when they thought they wouldn't survive a collapse, the shaking stopped. A deep silence settled over them, broken only by their uneven breathing.

"Is everyone okay?" Gil asked, scanning the group.

Lily pulled away from Chloe slightly, her hands trembling. "I'm fine."

Chloe nodded, but unease coiled in her stomach. "Me too."

"Did something feel odd about that tremor?" Yuki asked.

"It didn't feel very natural," Einar pointed out. "The timing was completely off."

Seraphine ran a hand along the chamber wall, her fingers tracing the symbols etched into the stone. "I think something was activated."

"The Eye?" Thalia asked, adjusting her glasses.

Seraphine exhaled slowly. "No, that thing would lead us to it," she said, pointing to the fragment in Chloe's hand. "I think it's the thing that's keeping it locked away. I think we're getting close."

She looked up contemplatively before raising her hand. "Come on, let's keep moving. The other agents could be back any minute."

The tunnels seemed to breathe with an eerie life of their own. The chilled air brushed past the group like whispers of warning, and the faint pulse of the obsidian fragment in Chloe's hand added an unusual rhythm to their steps. Despite the lingering tension from Lily's rescue, the group pressed on, united by an unspoken determination.

Chloe walked beside a still shaken Lily, her hand resting protectively on her sister's arm to steady her over the uneven ground. Seraphine led the way, her movements smooth and purposeful. Her old cloak swayed like an echoed shadow in the dim light.

"This way," Seraphine said, turning abruptly into another narrow passage. The air shifted, carrying a faint metallic tang. As they entered a small chamber with sleek, reflective walls, she halted and gestured for the group to stop.

"This will give us a moment to regroup," Seraphine said calmly.

Chloe led Lily to a stone ledge, brushing away dust before helping her to sit down. "How are you doing?" Chloe asked, her tone soft, her concern evident.

"I'm okay," Lily replied, though her voice was softly timid. Her eyes still hinted at fear, but Chloe could see that old resilience in them, nevertheless. "They didn't hurt me, but I heard things, Chloe. Raj kept talking about something called a convergence point. He said they need the Eye to align with a specific location to unlock its power. It's about control—over everything. And they're using these tunnels to move around, quickly."

Gil crouched beside Lily, his brow furrowed. "Did he mention where this convergence point is?"

Lily shook her head. "Just that it's tied to Upland's history."

Chloe took out her phone. "Let's ask Arthur about this and see what he says," she said, typing a text.

After a few minutes her phone buzzed with a reply from Arthur: *Convergence point. That aligns with the inscriptions—alignment, balance, destiny. If they activate the Eye in the right spot, it could exponentially amplify its power.,*

Chloe read out the message to the group.

Mei spread her notes across the chamber floor, focusing intently. "But where? Upland is filled with landmarks—Olive House, the Madonna of the Trail monument … It could be any of them."

"Or maybe all of them," Aoife suggested, turning to a clean page in her notebook. Her Irish accent softened as she thought aloud. "Think about it— alignment … If they're creating an alignment, these locations could all work in sync—each one enhancing the others."

"So what? They do something in each location to cause them to align?" Chloe asked, looking from one member of the crew to the other.

"It seems that way, but maybe there's a central control," Mei responded.

"Okay so how do we know where to go first?" Lily asked.

Luca, sitting nearby looking at his tablet, frowned. "There's increased activity near the Madonna of the Trail. I reckon we should start there. If that's their focus, we don't have much time."

Chloe looked at Seraphine, her voice steady. "Can we trust this lead?"

Seraphine met her gaze with confidence. "The Society doesn't waste effort. If they're concentrating on the monument, it's important."

Trust and Conflict

As the group was getting ready to leave, Yuki walked up to Seraphine, blocking her path, her stormy expression revealing there was still unspoken tension toward Seraphine. "How can we be sure you're not setting us up? You've been leading us into danger from the very beginning. And you just heard our plan, for all we know, you could be turning us in to The Society."

Seraphine answered slowly, her eyes calm yet firm. "You don't have to trust me … but consider this: Lily is alive because of me. I'm risking everything to be here. If you'd rather walk into The Society's clutches blindly, feel free to go on your own."

Before Yuki could fire back, Einar gently stepped between them, his presence providing a calming sense of strength. "Let's pause for a moment," he said gently. "We really don't have time for this right now."

Chloe joined him, putting her hand on Yuki's shoulder, "Yuki, I totally understand your misgivings. Really, I do. But we have to stay united if we're going to take down The Society. We need her right now."

Yuki clenched her jaw and then gave a reluctant nod. "Fine. But if she crosses the line …"

Seraphine's lips curled into a slight, humorless smile. "I wouldn't expect anything less."

The Convergence Point

After what seemed like hours, the tunnels inclining as they walked, the group finally emerged into crisp, fresh night air before the Madonna of the Trail monument. Its weathered stone gleamed softly in the moonlight, a solemn, unmoving guardian of her secrets. As they drew closer, Chloe noticed faint symbols etched into its base—softened and worn by time yet unmistakably similar to those in the tunnels.

"This is it," Chloe said, glancing at her phone as a message from Arthur appeared: *This monument wasn't just meant as a tribute; it was designed as a safeguard. Balance, protection, and alignment—it's all connected to the Eye.*

"As we thought, everything is connected," Chloe added as she read the message aloud.

"A safeguard for what?" Lily asked, her voice low.

"The Eye," Seraphine replied. "Or something connected to it. The Society must have recently realized its significance, which is why they're here now."

Chloe turned to Luca. "Can you check for signals? We need to find out if The Society is already here."

Luca adjusted his device, frowning as he worked. "Interference is strong, but I'm detecting movement near the Olive House—west of here." He exhaled sharply. "They've split their forces. We must act quickly."

Revelation and Sacrifice

Before the group could decide on their next move, a low rumble trembled the ground beneath them. The symbols at the base of the monument began to glow faintly, and with a grinding sound, stones slowly shifted apart in a section of the monument to reveal a narrow staircase spiraling downward.

This wasn't listed in any of the records, Arthur messaged when Chloe quickly told him. *It could lead to a chamber—perhaps even the Eye itself.*

Everyone glanced around, unsure what to do next.

Chloe's resolve hardened. "We go in."

"I'll stay here," Yuki said, her tone firm and leaving no room for argument.

Chloe hesitated, searching her face. "Are you sure?"

Yuki nodded. "If The Society shows up, someone has to hold them off. I can buy you some time."

Chloe placed a hand on her shoulder, worried. "Be careful …"

Yuki gave a small grin. "Always." Then she turned and melted into the shadows.

The rest of the group descended into the unknown. The air became cooler again and the stone walls more oppressive, etched with now familiar symbols that glowed faintly.

Reaching the bottom, it opened into a vast chamber, the ceiling adorned with intricate carvings that seemed to flow together, writhing as if alive. At the center stood a pedestal, another obsidian fragment on it, glowing eerily.

"It's beautiful," Lily whispered, stepping closer.

Arthur's text came moments later: *It seems that fragment is a key. It's connected to activating the Eye.*

"A key to what?" Mei asked, her voice filled with awe.

Before Arthur could respond, Luca's device crackled to life. Yuki's voice pierced through the static, strained and urgent. "They're here. Too many. I'll—"

The transmission ended abruptly.

Chloe's breath caught in her throat. "Yuki!" Her voice echoed off the chamber walls. Then—shocked silence.

Seraphine's expression darkened. "She understood the risk. If we don't complete this, her sacrifice will be in vain."

The Next Steps

The group stood frozen, caught between continuing the mission and returning for Yuki. The obsidian fragment on the pedestal pulsed brighter, sending ripples of light through the space and revealing new inscriptions carved into the walls.

Thalia traced some of them with her fingers, glancing around her, then, "It's a map!" she said. "It points to the Eye."

Chloe's fists clenched as she fought back tears. Her voice was steady, but her determination burned brightly. "Alright. Then we're getting close. We *will* finish this. For Yuki. For everyone The Society has harmed."

Chapter 18

Choices and Consequences

The chamber gently pulsed with the warm glow of the obsidian fragment, its soft light dancing upon the ancient walls and ceiling. Important choices waited ahead. Chloe found herself at the pedestal, holding onto its edge as if it could calm the whirlwind of thoughts swirling in her mind. The room was quiet, aside from a soothing, almost subliminal hum coming from both fragments now, yet the unmistakable tension among the team filled the air, creating a palpable connection.

Lily finally broke the silence, her voice trembling. "We can't just leave Yuki up there. She's fighting for us, but what are we doing? We don't even know if she's okay."

Chloe turned to her sister, her eyes calm. "She's giving us time to finish this, Lily. If we don't stop The

Society, then everything she's doing will be meaningless."

Lily clenched her fists. "But what if she—" Her voice broke. "What if she doesn't pull through?"

Einar stepped forward, his towering frame solid and reassuring. "Then we ensure her fight wasn't for nothing," he said gently. "Yuki knew what she was doing, and she wouldn't want us to throw everything away to come back for her."

From the corner of the room, Luca let out a frustrated sigh while tapping on his tablet. "Her signal's gone. The interference down here is insane. And let's be honest, The Society probably has jammers everywhere."

"Is that really all?" Lily asked, her frustration rising. "While she's up there putting in so much effort, you're just standing there?"

Thalia, who had been quietly studying the glowing map on the walls, turned to Lily. Her voice was steady, kind yet firm. "It's not about just shrugging our shoulders, Lily. If we rush back now, we'll all end up captured—or worse. Sometimes, the best way to honor someone's fight is to ensure it matters."

Lily's eyes filled with tears. "How can we just leave her behind?"

Chloe moved in closer and rested her hand softly on Lily's shoulder. "We won't leave her behind. We're going to complete the mission because her sacrifice deserves to mean something. That's what she would want us to do."

Seraphine, leaning casually against the wall, added, "Yuki's not the kind to give up easily. She understood the risks and made her choice. If you want to honor her, you should focus on the task at hand."

Gil's voice sliced through the mounting tension, calm yet resolute. "We can't separate again. If we want a chance to stop The Society, we need to stick together and keep moving forward."

Luca's tablet emitted a gentle ping, causing him to squint at the screen. "There's movement near the Olive House. It matches the convergence point on the map."

"That's where they're making the next move to activate the Eye," Seraphine said, her eyes flashing.

Thalia sat back, a gleeful expression on her face. "These tunnels connect *everything*. The last stop on this map is the Olive House. Which means—"

Einar cracked his knuckles, his voice steady. "It means we keep moving. Mission first."

Descent and Resolve

Having secured this new fragment, the group ventured deeper into the tunnels, resolutely following the glowing map's guidance. The temperature turned even cooler, and they could see their breaths creating soft puffs in the air as they navigated the narrow passages. The obsidian fragments lit up even more, their glow intensifying with each step, as if it were encouraging them to continue.

Thalia walked beside Chloe, her keen eyes glancing over the walls. "Look at these symbols!" she exclaimed, gesturing at the beautiful carvings. "They're not just guiding us; they also hold some important warnings. It seems the designer really wanted to create a puzzle for anyone unfamiliar with what to look for!"

"What kind of warnings?" Chloe asked, keeping her voice low.

Thalia traced her fingers over a faint marking. "If we take a wrong turn, we could end up somewhere we can't escape from. Or worse."

Aoife glanced over, sketching the markings into her journal. "It's like breadcrumbs, but some of the crumbs lead to traps instead of the path. We need to stay sharp."

Gil, walking just behind them, chuckled softly. "So basically, don't trust anything. Got it."

Thalia smirked slightly. "Glad you're paying attention."

Ahead of them, Lily hesitated, her voice breaking the quiet. "Do you think The Society really believes the Eye is as powerful as they say?"

Arthur's voice came through once more, calm and steady: *Legends like this always begin with a grain of truth. If the Eye can amplify energy as we believe it can, it's more dangerous than any of us ever realized.*

Chloe quickened her pace. "Then we have to stop them. No matter what it takes."

Gil matched her step, his voice reassuring. "And we will. One step at a time. And if there's any chance to help Yuki, we'll take it."

Another Puzzle

The tunnel opened into another spacious chamber, the air humming with an unusual energy. At the center of the room stood an ancient mechanism—a series of rotating discs adorned with intricate symbols.

"It looks like our next challenge," Mei said, stepping forward to examine the mechanism. She ran her fingers over the carvings, her brow furrowed in concentration. "If we align these symbols with the map, it should open the way forward."

Chloe leaned closer, studying the discs. "Can you figure it out?"

"How do you know me? Of course. It may take a while—"

Before Mei could add anything further, Luca's tablet emitted a sharp beep. His face turned pale as he gazed at the screen. "Uh, guys? We've got company. They've discovered another route into the tunnels, and they're moving quickly."

The faint sound of footsteps and voices echoed from the distance, growing louder with each second.

Thalia's voice pierced through the rising tension, steady and purposeful. "Mei, focus on the puzzle. The rest of us need to establish some kind of defense. If they reach us before we're done, this is going to get messy."

Chloe faced the group, her voice steady and strong. "We solve this puzzle and keep going. No matter what happens, we won't stop."

The obsidian fragments glowed brighter, casting long, flickering shadows across the room as the team prepared for the inevitable fight.

Chapter 19

The Final Puzzle

The chamber shimmered with the soft, steady glow of the obsidian fragments, their light casting long shadows on the walls. The massive mechanism blocking their path loomed before them, its rotating discs etched with intricate, faintly glowing symbols. Chloe stood at the center of the group, her phone buzzing in her hand as Arthur's latest message appeared.

The mechanism resembles a puzzle. If the discs aren't aligned correctly, it could trigger a defense—possibly catastrophic. Be precise.

"Great," Chloe muttered, glancing at the group. "Arthur says we need to be precise. Or else. No pressure or anything."

Mei crouched beside the mechanism, her brow furrowed as she traced the symbols with her fingertips.

"These are constellations—Orion, Lyra, Cygnus … If we rotate them in the correct order, we should be able to unlock it."

"And if we don't?" Lily asked, leaning over Mei's shoulder.

Luca chimed in, his gaze focused on his tablet. "Maybe it's best if we don't explore that right now. There's a secondary lock linked to the discs, and I'm working on deciphering it, but this gadget is a bit tricky to handle!"

Arthur's next text appeared on Chloe's screen: *Be very careful with the order. A single mistake could collapse the tunnel—or worse.*

"Fantastic," Lily said with a nervous giggle. "Yeah, no pressure at all."

"Orion first," Mei said, brushing aside the tension as she carefully rotated one of the discs. A faint click echoed through the chamber.

A Race Against Time

From somewhere behind them, hurried footsteps echoed through the tunnels, growing louder.

Chloe's phone buzzed again. Arthur's message read: *That noise—The Society is close. You need to hurry.*

Seraphine turned sharply, her posture tensing. "They're coming." She moved toward the entrance, her hand resting on the hilt of her blade. "Einar, let's slow them down."

Einar nodded, his large frame striding toward the narrow corridor. With a grunt, he swung his weapon at the supports of the entrance. The resounding crash sent debris tumbling, temporarily blocking the path and muffling the sound of the pursuit.

"Well, that should give us some time," Seraphine said, brushing dust off her shoulders. "But not a lot."

"Keep working!" Chloe urged, but calm, controlled.

The Final Alignment

Luca's tablet emitted a soft beep, and he raised a hand to capture their attention. "Wait! There's a secondary lock. If the discs aren't perfectly aligned, it could trigger a trap. I think I can bypass it, but I need a few minutes."

"We don't have a minute," Seraphine said sharply, glancing toward the blocked corridor.

Mei turned another disc, her fingers moving steadily. "Orion here … Lyra next …"

Chloe looked at her phone as another message from Arthur came in: *Cygnus is the last. But in reverse.*

"Cygnus is next, in *reverse*" Chloe relayed, her voice steady.

Mei nodded as she carefully aligned the final disc.

"What happens if we mess up?" Lily asked, her voice barely above a whisper.

Arthur's reply came immediately: *You really don't want to know.*

"Helpful," Lily muttered, crossing her arms.

Thalia knelt beside Mei, her tone encouraging. "You're almost there. Just one more—nice and easy."

Mei took a deep breath and twisted the last disc counterclockwise. A soft vibration pulsed through the stone as the final disc settled into place. One final click, followed by a deep, mechanical hum ….

The Hidden Chamber

The wall in front of them shuddered before sliding open, revealing a hidden chamber. The soft, rhythmic glow of a larger obsidian fragment lit up the space. It sat atop a pedestal, its pulse perfectly synchronized with the smaller fragments Chloe was still carrying.

This is it, Arthur texted. *Another piece of the Eye. Be careful—it could be more powerful than we realize.*

Mei stepped closer, her fingers gliding over the inscriptions carved into the pedestal. "These writings are … different. They speak of balance, not control."

"What does that mean?" Lily asked, stepping forward cautiously.

Arthur's next message arrived quickly: *The Eye wasn't designed for domination—it was intended to stabilize. It amplifies intention. Whoever wields it can shape reality according to their desires.*

Chloe's stomach tightened. "So, if The Society gets this …"

"They'll reshape the world however they want," Seraphine said grimly.

"Total control," Einar rumbled, his tone dark.

Taking a Stand

Before anyone could say anything more, the ground beneath their feet shuddered violently. Cracks snaked across the chamber walls as this fragment's glow intensified, its pulsing light casting sharp, jagged shadows around them.

"What's happening?" Chloe shouted, gripping the pedestal for balance.

Arthur's message popped up on her phone: *The fragment is reacting. The Society might be nearer than you realize.*

The sound of voices shouting and pounding footsteps grew louder, echoing ominously through the tunnels.

Seraphine drew her weapon, a fierce expression on her face. "If they arrive while it's active …"

"We won't allow that," Chloe said, her voice steady and unwavering.

Thalia stepped forward, calm yet commanding. "Mei and Luca, find out what's going on with the fragment. Einar, Gil, and Seraphine—we'll secure the entrance."

Chloe turned to face the group, her eyes blazing with determination. "We stand our ground. Whatever it takes, we won't let them get this."

Chapter 20

The Battle for Control

The chamber shuddered under the weight of distant footsteps, each echo growing louder as The Society approached. Dust floated from cracks in the ceiling, glinting in the eerie, pulsing glow of the obsidian fragments. Chloe glanced at her phone as another text from Arthur buzzed onto the screen:

They're almost there. Hold the line. Do whatever it takes to protect the fragments.

Seraphine, already stationed at the entrance of the chamber, tightened her grip on her blade. "They'll strike us hard and fast. Stay alert."

Einar lifted a hefty piece of debris and placed it near the passage to form a makeshift barricade. "Let them come," he said with calm confidence. "They won't get past us."

Gil stepped forward, standing shoulder to shoulder with Chloe. His dark eyes were focused and steady. "He's right. We'll hold them off, but we need to be smart. Einar, keep blocking the main entrance. Seraphine, support him. Chloe and I will handle the distractions. Everyone else, stay with the fragment."

Mei quickly snapped photos of the inscriptions near the pedestal, her hands moving precisely. "These carvings might help us determine how to control—or destroy—the fragment," she said, her voice urgent but focused.

Chloe's phone buzzed again. A message from Arthur read: *Focus on the symbols. Groups of three may indicate an overload mechanism. Stay cautious.*

"Got it," Chloe murmured, passing the information along.

Luca glanced up from his tablet, a concerned expression on his face. "I've got some unfortunate news. Their group is splitting up. One team is heading right towards us, while the other is approaching from the side."

Gil didn't flinch. "Then we hold them here. If we can keep the main group busy, the flanking team will have to regroup instead of attacking."

The Society Attacks

The chamber burst into chaos as agents from The Society stormed through the entrance. Their dark uniforms blended with the shadows, their movements quick and calculated. At the front of the group stood Raj, his commanding voice cutting through the commotion.

"Get the fragment!" he shouted. "No mercy!"

Einar charged forward, swinging his makeshift weapon with precise, crushing blows.

The impacts shattered bone and sent enemy figures sprawling, their cries lost in the battle. Another rushed him, but he met them with a brutal shoulder-check, knocking them backward before bringing his weapon down with a sickening crunch.

Seraphine moved quickly, weaving through the fight. A Society agent lunged at her but she sidestepped effortlessly, spun, and drove her dagger into their side before they could react. She didn't pause to watch them fall. "You're outnumbered," Raj called, his piercing eyes locking onto Chloe. "Hand over the fragment, and I might let you live."

Chloe leveled a furious look at him, her voice firm. "Not a chance."

Raj smirked, stepping closer. "Still so stubborn. Just like your father."

The words struck Chloe like a punch on the gut.

Her father.

Her breath caught as memories of her father flooded her mind—his unshakable determination and belief in doing what was right. Grief and anger swirled within her, threatening to overwhelm her.

"What do you know about my father?" she hissed, her heart pounding.

Raj's smile twisted cruelly. "More than you think. He stood in our way, too. Look where it got him."

Gil stepped between them, his voice calm yet firm. "Don't let him get to you. He's trying to throw you off. Stay focused on the mission."

Chloe forced herself to breathe. Raj was trying to distract her. She shook her head, struggling to suppress her emotions. "Lily, stay with Mei and safeguard the fragment."

Lily hesitated, glancing between Chloe and Raj, but then nodded.

The Fragment Reacts

As the battle raged on, the larger obsidian fragment started to glow more intensely. Its rhythmic pulse quickened, filling the chamber with an even louder, unsettling hum. The smaller fragments Chloe still carried were also pulsing.

"What's happening?" Lily shouted, shielding her eyes from the intense light.

Chloe's phone buzzed again. Arthur's message said: *The fragments are responding to the conflict. They're drawing from the energy of the emotions and intentions surrounding them.*

"Can we stop it?" Mei asked, hurriedly snapping more photos of the inscriptions.

Arthur's response came almost immediately: *Not unless you completely understand it—and you're running out of time.*

Raj's face lit up with triumph as he lunged toward the pedestal. "It's awakening!" he shouted. "The Eye's power will be mine!"

Seraphine intercepted him with a snarl, their blades colliding in a shower of sparks. "Not today," she hissed, sending him flying back with a vicious kick.

A Hard Choice

The large fragment's glow rapidly grew stronger, engulfing the chamber in blinding light. Cracks spread across the walls, and the ground shook violently beneath their feet.

Chloe's phone buzzed with another urgent text: *There's an overload mechanism. If triggered, it will destroy the fragment, but someone must activate it manually.*

Her voice wavered as she conveyed the message to the team. "We have to destroy it. If we don't, the Society will use it to control everything."

Arthur's reply appeared: *Destroying it means losing the chance to understand its full power. What if it could be used for good?*

When Chloe relayed his response, Seraphine's voice cut through the chaos. "That's a risk we can't take. It's too dangerous for anyone to manage safely."

Gil stepped forward, his tone firm. "Arthur, explain how to trigger the overload. If there's any safe way to do it, we'll attempt it. If not, we destroy it now."

Arthur responded quickly: *Look for three overlapping symbols. They will indicate the trigger point.*

Chloe examined the pedestal and discovered the markings. Her heart raced as she reached for the mechanism. Just as she was about to act, Raj broke free from Seraphine's hold and lunged at her.

Einar tackled him hard, pinning him to the ground. "Go!" Einar shouted. "Do what you have to do—I've got him!"

The Sacrifice

Chloe quickly aligned the engravings on the mechanism. The chamber resonated with a deafening hum as the fragment burst apart in a flash of blinding light. The shockwave knocked everyone off balance.

Raj screamed in rage as the force threw him back. Disoriented, the Society's agents began to retreat.

The ground shook violently, sending stones raining down from above as cracks spread across the ceiling.

"We need to go!" Gil shouted, grabbing Chloe's arm.

Einar stood firm near the collapsing entrance, his expression calm. "I'll cover your escape, stop Raj. Go now!"

"No!" Lily cried, her voice breaking. "We can get out together!"

Gil held Chloe back as she tried to move toward Einar. "He's right. We need to leave, Chloe."

Tears streamed down Chloe's face as she looked back at Einar. Her voice cracked. "Oh Einar …Thank you … for everything."

Einar gave her a faint smile. "Go. Protect them."

The team ran toward the surface as the chamber collapsed behind them. Dust and debris filled the air, and the sound of Raj's furious screams faded into the rubble.

Aftermath

The team stood quietly under the early morning light, gazing at the sealed tunnel entrance.

Chloe clenched her fists, her voice shaking and tears streaming down her face. "I can't believe we've lost another person."

Gil placed a hand on her shoulder, his voice raw but steady. "We'll miss him. He was a noble friend. It was an incredible sacrifice."

Lily held Chloe in a tight hug, her face also wet with tears. "We'll make this count. We'll stop The Society—for Einar. For everyone."

Chapter 21

Regrouping and Revelations

The morning sun bathed the sky in soft hues of orange and pink as the team trudged silently toward safety. The streets of Upland were quiet, but the weight of their mission, the loss of Yuki and Einar's sacrifice made every step feel heavier. The fresh air carried hints of dew and earth, though no one noticed. They were lost in thought, each bearing their own burden of grief and determination.

Chloe walked to the front of the group, her eyes fixed on the horizon, but her mind was far away. She couldn't shake the image of Einar's calm face as he urged them to leave him behind. Her heart ached with guilt and loss.

Gil walked beside her, his gaze shifting between her and the path ahead. Finally, he spoke, his voice steady yet firm. "Chloe, you made the right choice."

She looked at him, her voice soft and hesitant. "Did I? He's gone because of me."

Gil shook his head. "Einar knew what he was doing. He gave us a chance to keep fighting. He wouldn't want you to blame yourself."

Chloe sighed, her shoulders hunched tightly. "It doesn't make it any easier."

Lily, walking just behind them, caught up and slipped her arm around Chloe. "Einar believed in us. We can't let him down. We have to finish this—for him."

Chloe nodded, drawing strength from her sister's words. "We will."

The Safehouse

Hidden behind overgrown bushes and cracked fences, the safehouse resembled nothing more than an old, neglected home. Its peeling paint and sagging roof provided no hint of the vital role it played.

Inside, the air was cool and still, faint scents of aged wood and dust, and stale coffee wafted around. The silence provided comfort after the chaos they had escaped.

Seraphine nodded, looking around, her eyes scanning the room. "This is a good place to regroup. Let's take a moment to breathe, but don't take too long. We don't have time to waste."

Mei and Arthur quickly arranged their notes and the shattered pieces of the obsidian fragments at the dining table. Luca dropped onto the couch, his fingers already flying over his tablet as he monitored communications.

Chloe sank into a chair, resting her head in her hands.

Lily pulled up a chair next to her, placing a reassuring hand on Chloe's arm. "You're not alone in this," she said gently. "Let us help."

Chloe glanced at her sister, noticing the strength and determination in her eyes. "I can't bear to lose anyone else," she whispered.

"And we won't," Lily said firmly. "We're stronger now, we've learned so much and we're making progress. We'll figure this out."

Across the room, Aoife stood by a dusty bookshelf, flipping through her notebook. "If we're going to stay ahead of The Society, we need to understand what we're up against. That latest fragment contains more secrets than we realize."

Analyzing the Fragment

At the dining table, Arthur's voice shattered the silence. "I believe I've discovered something," he said, leaning over the latest fragment Chloe had managed to keep.

Mei, sitting next to him, leaned in closer. "It's not merely decoration—it's a coded message. These carvings are instructions."

Thalia joined them, her sharp eyes scanning the markings. "Instructions for what?"

Arthur adjusted his glasses. "It looks like a map. Another piece of the Eye is hidden close by."

"Another map? Where?" Chloe asked, standing and moving closer.

Mei pointed to one of the carvings. "The Olive House. Remember there was reference to it in the chamber too. It's been right under our noses this whole time. This confirms it."

Luca glanced up from his tablet. "That makes sense. The Society has been concentrating their efforts in that area for weeks. They must know something we don't."

Aoife added thoughtfully, "It's not just about location. The Olive House might be part of something bigger—a network of places connected to the Eye's power."

A sudden knock at the door made everyone freeze, their hearts racing. Seraphine raised a hand, motioning for everyone to be quiet. Tension filled the air as she cautiously approached the door, her blade poised and ready for anything that might come next.

Yuki's Return

"It's me," came a familiar, tired voice.

"Yuki?" Chloe rushed forward as Seraphine opened the door.

Yuki stumbled in, her clothes torn and her face pale, yet her expression held a hint of a smile. "Miss me?" she joked, collapsing into a chair.

Lily rushed to her side, her hands shaking. "We thought we had lost you."

"Not yet," Yuki said, her voice faint but steady. "But I've got news. The Society is regrouping at the

Olive House. Whatever they're planning, it's happening soon."

Seraphine nodded, "So we've gathered." Her expression softened a bit. "It's nice to see you made it."

The Plan

"Alright team, with Yuki here, it's time for a plan. Gather around," Arthur said, gesturing them over to the dinner table.

Everyone came together at the table, temporarily setting aside their exhaustion.

"We split up," Arthur started, "Mei and I will continue working on the fragment's message. Luca, you keep an eye on communications and watch for any movement. The rest of you need to scout the Olive House and determine what The Society is planning."

Gil frowned, his arms crossed. "Splitting up is dangerous. Are you sure that's the right move?"

"We don't have a choice," Chloe said. "If we wait, they'll get to whatever's there before us."

Aoife nodded, agreeing, "If we're careful, we can collect what we need without attracting too much attention. But we'll have to move fast."

Thalia crossed her arms. "It's risky, but it might work. Just ensure we have a clear exit strategy."

Lily spoke softly, "Promise me we'll all come back. No one else gets left behind."

Chloe locked eyes with her sister, "We'll come back. All of us."

The Going gets Tougher

Later, after everyone had something to eat and rested up a little, Luca's tablet beeped. His face went pale as he read the information on the screen.

"They're sending reinforcements," he stated. "If we're not cautious, we'll be walking into a trap."

Chloe tightened her grip on the bag she was packing in preparation to move out, her expression unyielding. "Then we turn the trap on them. This ends now."

When they were ready, the team exchanged determined looks before leaving the safehouse, each step about to take them closer to the next confrontation that lay ahead.

Chapter 22

The Olive House Infiltration

The night air was throbbing with tension as the team approached the Olive House. Its weathered wooden frame loomed like a relic from another era, surrounded by gnarled, skeletal trees that clawed at the moonlit sky. The cracked windows reflected a faint silvery light, making the house seem alive, as if it were watching them.

Chloe raised her hand, signaling everyone to stop before they crossed the property line. She exhaled shakily. "This feels like the beginning of every haunted house story ever."

"It's meant to feel that way," Seraphine said softly, crouching low as she surveyed the yard. "Fear keeps people away. It's The Society's specialty."

Lily, standing close to Chloe, glanced nervously at the house. "Well, they're doing a great job. This place gives me chills."

"Chills or not, we're going in," Gil said, adjusting the strap of his laptop bag. His voice was steady yet authoritative. "Stick to the plan: get in, gather intel, and get out. No unnecessary risks."

"Motion sensors," Yuki murmured, pointing to the west side of the house. "I can disable them, but we'll have to move fast."

"Luca, are you picking up anything else?" Chloe asked, turning toward him.

Luca's fingers danced across his tablet as he scanned for signals. "They're definitely using some kind of jammer nearby. I can't break through yet, but I'll keep trying. Just keep me covered."

Thalia crouched next to Yuki, her sharp eyes observing the setup. "If this is their main base now, they've definitely set traps inside. Be prepared for anything."

Chloe nodded. "All right, everyone. Let's do this."

The Infiltration

Yuki moved swiftly, dismantling the motion sensors with practiced ease. A soft click signaled her success, and she gestured for the team to advance.

Chloe gently pushed open a side door, cringing a bit as it let out a loud, long creak. The group froze, holding their breaths as they listened for any signs of movement. When all remained quiet, they quietly slipped inside, hearts racing with anticipation.

The interior was just as unsettling as the exterior. Dust covered every surface, and cobwebs hung in the corners like neglected curtains. The peeling wallpaper appeared to droop under the weight of years, and a faint smell of mildew lingered in the air.

"This place feels sooo spooky," Lily whispered, cozying up to Chloe. Her flashlight danced across the faded gaze of an old portrait, which hung a little askew on the wall.

"Keep your wits about you," Seraphine encouraged. "The Society loves its drama, but remember, it's all just smoke and mirrors. Let's concentrate on what truly matters."

Aoife ran her fingers along the wall as they moved, examining its texture. "This house is older than it appears. There might be hidden passages—something we could use if we need to escape."

At the end of a long hallway, they found a staircase leading down to who knew what.

Gil pointed toward it. "If they're hiding anything important, it's down there."

"Then let's find out," Chloe said, gripping her flashlight tightly as they descended.

Discovering The Society's Plans

The basement was surprisingly pristine, a vast contrast to the worn-out house above. Shelves neatly lined the walls, filled with carefully arranged files and unique artifacts. Tables showcased an array of blueprints, maps, and important documents. In the heart of the room stood a metal casket, beautifully engraved with glowing symbols that gently pulsed with light.

"This is it," Seraphine said, her voice barely above a whisper. "Everything they're planning is right here."

Gil scanned the table, flipping through the papers with sharp, practiced movements. "They're targeting Upland's landmarks—the Madonna of the Trail, the olive groves, and even Mt. Baldy. They're using these locations to amplify the Eye's power."

"That makes sense," Yuki said, examining a blueprint. "If they align it properly, they could control everything—resources, politics, even people."

Chloe gazed at the glowing casket. "And what about this?"

"It looks like it's part of the Eye," Seraphine stated. "Or something that connects to it. If they intend to use it, we either take it or destroy it."

Mei leaned in closer, tracing the glowing symbols on the casket. "Destroying it might activate a failsafe. Taking it will slow them down, but it's risky either way."

Lily moved next to Chloe, her voice trembling slightly. "If this thing is so important, why would they leave it unguarded?"

"They wouldn't," Thalia said with a grim look, her eyes narrowing. "This feels like a trap."

The Hidden Threat

As Gil bent down to examine the casket, Yuki froze and raised a hand. "Wait," she whispered. "We're not alone."

The team fell quiet, straining to listen. The faint creak of floorboards above sent a chill down their spines.

"They've been watching us," Seraphine said, her voice low. She unsheathed her blade, her eyes narrowing. "Agents are upstairs. They were waiting for us to discover this."

"They're sealing us in," Luca said, glancing at his tablet. "We need to move. Quickly."

"They're coming down," Aoife said, positioning herself near a corner. "We'll need to fight our way out."

Moments later, the first agent emerged at the top of the stairs, his uniform blending with the shadows. More agents followed, their movements deliberate. A tall man with a scar on his cheek stepped into view, his presence commanding.

"You didn't think it would be this easy, did you?" he sneered, his voice filled with sarcasm.

Chloe stepped forward, her voice steady. "You're not getting what you came for."

The man's smirk deepened. "Oh, I think we will." He gestured, and his agents surged forward, more descending the stairs.

A Chaotic Escape

The room became a swirl of mayhem. Seraphine and Yuki moved like a well-practiced team, their strikes swift and precise. Seraphine's blade flashed in the dim light, slicing through the air as she ducked under an enemy's wild swing and countered with a sharp, precise stab to their shoulder. The agent cried out, stumbling back, but another rushed in to take his place.

Yuki was already moving, blocking an incoming strike with a swift parry before pivoting and driving her knee hard into an attacker's gut. He doubled over, and she finished him with a quick, brutal elbow to the temple. Another enemy lunged at her from behind, but Seraphine was there, spinning low and slicing a deep cut across the attacker's leg.

Across the room, Aoife used her strength to shove a towering heavy shelf into the path of advancing agents. It toppled forward, crashing into the advancing agents with a deafening boom. A cloud of dust exploded into the air, and for a brief moment, the attackers were trapped behind the fallen barrier.

Meanwhile, Gil and Chloe worked quickly in sync to shift the casket toward the far wall.

"We're running out of time!" Gil shouted over the noise.

Nearby, "This way!" Yuki shouted, pushing aside a loose panel she'd found, to uncover a hidden tunnel.

The team rushed into the narrow passage, carrying the casket along with them. The cold and damp air hit them instantly, and their footsteps echoed loudly off the close stone walls.

Behind them, the agents were already recovering, climbing over the debris, weapons drawn.

"They're gaining on us," Luca warned, glancing back.

Seraphine stopped abruptly and turned to face the pursuing agents. Her blade glinted in the faint light of the tunnel. "Go," she said firmly. "I'll hold them off."

"No!" Chloe protested, her voice breaking.

Seraphine gave her a faint smile. "This is what I do. Go. Finish this."

Before Chloe could argue, Seraphine turned and disappeared into the shadows as the team raced forward and burst out of the tunnel into the fresh night air, their hearts hammering. Behind them, the distant sounds of combat echoed faintly, as the reality of the situation settled on them, Seraphine's sacrifice a haunting reminder of the Einar's.

Safe, for now

Chloe held on to her end of the casket tightly, her knuckles white. "We can't leave her behind."

Gil placed a steady hand on her shoulder, his voice calm yet firm. "We'll return for her. For now, let's get out of here, regroup and figure out our next move."

Lily moved next to Chloe, her voice gentle yet firm. "We must go Chloe. We'll get this done. For her—and for everyone these evil people are harming."

The team exchanged determined looks before moving into the night, ready for whatever lay ahead.

Chapter 23

Secrets Beneath the Gazebo

The next afternoon the safehouse buzzed with quiet activity. The faint hum of Luca's laptop mingled with the rustling of papers as Arthur and Mei pored over their notes. Chloe sat at the table, her fingers lightly tracing the edges of the metal casket they had retrieved from the Olive House. It felt heavier than it should have, weighed down not only by its secrets but also by the memory of Seraphine's sacrifice.

Yuki paced nearby, her voice shattering the silence. "We can't leave her out there," she said, sharp yet concerned. "She's one of us now."

"We'll get her back," Chloe said, her tone steady despite the tight grip she held on the edge of the table. "But we have to be smart about it. The Society isn't going to let us just walk in and take her."

Gil leaned against the window frame, his calm voice reassuring. "Seraphine is clearly an old hand at this. She gave us time to figure this out. We owe it to her to make the most of the advantage she's given us."

Mei looked up from her work, her face alight with discovery. "This casket isn't just a container. The inscriptions match those from the fragment. It's a key to something."

Arthur nodded, adjusting his glasses as he examined the carvings. "It's supposed to activate or unlock something, possibly another part of the Eye."

Luca, sitting on the couch, suddenly perked up. "I've intercepted some Society chatter. They're setting up downtown—at the Gibson Senior Center."

Chloe frowned. "Why there?"

"It's central and public," Yuki explained, already working through possibilities in her mind. "They can stage something big without raising too much suspicion."

Chloe stood, tying her hair into a ponytail. "Before we investigate the senior center, we need to check out the gazebo. If this key activates something, it's there." She stabbed a finger at the map that had guided them well up this point. The gazebo sat at another nexus point.

Chloe grabbed her jacket, slinging it over her shoulders as the group exchanged glances. No one needed to say it—they were running out of time.

Luca shut his laptop with a quiet snap, pushing himself off the couch. "I'll keep monitoring their chatter on my tablet while we move. If anything shifts, I'll let you know."

Gil nodded, already heading for the door. "Let's move—fast. We don't know how long we have before The Society makes their next move."

The Gazebo's Secret

The streets were quiet, the occasional thrum of distant traffic the only sound breaking the stillness. Their footsteps fell in sync, purposeful yet cautious, as they made their way toward the gazebo.

Streetlights flickered to life, casting pools of golden light onto the pavement. Chloe tightened her ponytail as she walked, her mind already working through the possibilities.

As the group approached the gazebo, the sky was streaked with shades of orange and purple, the last light of dusk fading. The white wooden structure stood quietly in the town square, its charm enhanced by fairy lights leftover from a recent local festival. To an outsider, it resembled any other quaint landmark.

"This feels … strange," Lily said softly, sticking close to Chloe. Her eyes darted around the square.

Chloe nodded. "The map from the fragment indicates this location. If The Society has been active downtown, this place must be more significant than it appears."

Yuki knelt near the gazebo, her fingers running over the wooden slats. "The foundation isn't solid. It's hollow underneath."

Gil joined her, crouching to examine the boards. He took out a multi-tool and worked swiftly. "There's a hatch. Just a moment …"

With a satisfying click, a concealed panel slid open, revealing a narrow staircase descending into darkness.

"Of course, there's a secret staircase," Yuki said with a smirk. "The Society never skips the classics."

Chloe gave her a small smile. "Let's stay focused. No one goes off alone."

Beneath the Gazebo

The staircase spiraled down into a chamber that smelled of damp earth and rusty metal. Shelves lined the walls with ancient books, scrolls, and peculiar artifacts. In the center of the room stood a pedestal, its surface intricately carved with designs that glowed faintly as they entered.

"This is it," Mei whispered, her fingers gliding over the carvings. "The key fits here."

Chloe passed the casket to Arthur, who gently set it on the pedestal. As the glowing designs flickered to life, they filled the chamber with a warm, pulsating light. A hum of energy filled the air while a section of the wall gracefully slid open, unveiling another intricate map etched into the stone.

Arthur leaned in, his eyes widening. "This isn't just about Upland," he said, pointing at the map. "It links to other locations—Israel, Ireland, Japan, Iceland … lots of them—places connected to ancient power."

"But for now, it leads to the senior center," Mei said, tracing a line with her finger. "Whatever's happening there is crucial."

The Society Mobilizes

Luca's tablet buzzed urgently. He glanced at the screen, his expression tightening. "The Society's on the move. They're converging on the senior center, setting up equipment. It seems like they're preparing for something big."

Chloe felt a knot twist in her stomach. "Then we have to stop them. Whatever they're planning, we can't let it happen."

"We need a distraction," Yuki said, checking her equipment. "They'll be watching every angle."

"I can create interference," Gil said, tossing his bag over his shoulder. "It won't last long, but it'll provide us a window."

Thalia adjusted her flashlight. "Once we get inside, we need to figure out what they're doing—and how to stop it—quickly."

"We stick to the plan," Chloe said, her voice firm. "Work together, cover each other, and don't take unnecessary risks."

Aoife nodded, her Irish lilt calm and steady. "And if it's as bad as it seems, we hit them hard. No second chances."

Beware!

As they prepared to leave, the pedestal in the chamber let out a faint hum. The glowing map on the wall shifted, and a new symbol emerged—a jagged, unfamiliar marking that seemed to pulse.

"What is *that?*" Lily asked, her voice trembling.

Arthur stepped closer, examining the symbol with a furrowed brow. "It looks like a warning. Whatever's happening at the senior center is more serious than we thought."

Chloe tightened her grip on her bag, her eyes blazing. "Let's go!"

SENIOR CENTER

Chapter 24

Confrontation at the Senior Center

The Gibson Senior Center sat in the heart of downtown Upland, its cheerful exterior at odds with the sinister activity inside. From their van parked a block away, the team quietly observed the bustling movement of The Society's agents through the windows.

Inside the brightly lit hall, a mysterious machine glowed an eerie blue as technicians worked around it with an urgency that hinted at something dangerous.

"They're running a tight operation," Yuki murmured, lowering her binoculars. "There are guards at every entrance, and that tech setup looks … advanced. This isn't just for show."

Gil leaned over Luca's shoulder, watching the live feed on his tablet. "They've sped up their plans. Someone's taken charge since Raj is gone, and they're not wasting any time."

Chloe's eyes were locked on the building, her mind racing. "Then we won't waste time either. Yuki and Luca take out their surveillance and comms. Mei and Arthur, stay here and keep monitoring the artifact readings. Gil and I will head inside to figure out what they're planning."

Lily crossed her arms. "What about me?!"

Chloe turned to her younger sister, softening her tone. "We need someone who can keep the team united from this point on. If anything happens, you'll be our anchor."

Lily hesitated, biting her lip, then nodded. "Alright, but promise me you'll be careful."

Chloe smiled, placing a hand on Lily's shoulder. "We will. I promise."

Sneaking In

Yuki and Luca slipped out first, their movements quiet and skillful. Yuki disabled the external cameras, whilst Luca, tapping into the agents' radio frequencies, fed them confusing static-laced misinformation.

"You're all set," Yuki said over comms. "But hurry. They'll catch on to the blackout soon."

Chloe and Gil entered through a side door, where the faint hum of the building's machinery blended with muffled voices. Inside, the atmosphere inside was charged, the glow of the machine visible even from where they stood.

Crouching behind the stacked crates, they peered into the main hall. The glowing blue device stood at the center, surrounded by Society agents and technicians who were tapping furiously at laptops and adjusting controls.

"It feels like they've ramped everything up since the explosion," Chloe whispered.

Gil nodded. "They're trying to salvage their plan. If we can disable that machine, we can slow them down—or maybe even stop them altogether."

A New Leader

A sharp, shrill, commanding voice shattered the tense silence. "Move faster. We're behind schedule, and failure is not an option."

Chloe shifted slightly to see the speaker. A tall woman in a sleek black uniform, with shortly cropped hair, strode into the hall, her presence both authoritative and intimidating. Her dark eyes scanned the room, missing nothing.

"Who's that?" Gil asked in a hushed voice.

"I don't know," Chloe said, narrowing her eyes. "But she's obviously in charge now."

"Dr. Anaya," one of the technicians called out nervously. "The machine is stabilizing. We're ready for the final sequence."

Dr. Anaya's sharp features softened slightly, but her voice remained cold. "Good. The Eye's power must be harnessed tonight. We can't afford another delay."

An Unexpected Ally

As Chloe and Gil planned their next move, a noise from a nearby room caught Chloe's attention. She signaled for Gil to follow, and they quietly approached the sound.

Inside, they discovered Seraphine sitting bound to a chair, struggling to get loose, her face showing signs of bruising, but her spirit clearly unbroken and defiant.

"Seraphine!" Chloe whispered, rushing to untie her.

Seraphine smirked faintly. "Took you long enough," she muttered, her voice raspy yet still carrying its characteristic sarcasm.

"What happened?" Gil asked, cutting through the ropes.

"They wrestled me down me at the Olive House," Seraphine said, flexing her sore wrists. "They thought I would break, but I played along while memorizing everything I could."

"What did you learn?" Chloe asked.

Seraphine looked grim. "Dr. Anaya knows they're vulnerable. That machine is everything. If we take it out now, they won't recover."

The Sabotage

Using Seraphine's intel, the three moved back towards the main hall. Chloe heard Dr. Anaya say, her tone leaving no room for argument. "Ensure nothing interrupts this."

As she strode out of the hall, Chloe let out a slow breath. "That's our window."

Gil and Chloe moved first, drawing the guards away from the machine by knocking over supply crates, creating a loud, clattering distraction. The guards, weapons drawn, rushed to investigate.

Seraphine moved fast, sliding into place at the console. "This system is more advanced than I anticipated," she murmured, her fingers moving skillfully over the keyboard. "When I trigger the shutdown, it'll short-circuit the whole system, but it won't be quiet."

"We'll handle any chaos, do it" Chloe urged.

As Seraphine entered the final commands, the machine's hum transformed into a piercing whine. Red lights flashed, alarms blared, and the guards came rushing back.

Dr. Anaya burst into the room, her face twisted in anger. "Stop them!" she screamed.

The Confrontation

More agents flooded the hall, weapons ready. Chloe and Gil opened fire, their aim precise as they protected Seraphine who continued inputting the final override.

"You're too late!" Dr. Anaya shouted above the noise. "Even if you destroy this machine, you can't stop the Eye's awakening. Its power is inevitable."

Chloe ducked behind cover, her breath rapid. "Your predecessor mentioned something similar," she shot back. "He's not around anymore."

Dr. Anaya's lips curled into a cold sneer. "Raj underestimated you. I won't make the same mistake."

"We'll stop you," Chloe stated, her voice steady. "Just like we did with him."

Overload

Suddenly, the machine emitted a high-pitched screech. The blue light intensified, casting harsh shadows throughout the room.

"What's happening?" Gil shouted, shielding his face.

Seraphine whirled around, her expression serious. "It's overloading. The entire building is going to explode. We need to get out—now!"

Chloe shouted over her comms. "Yuki, Luca, get out! This place is going to blow!"

Another Quick Escape

The team sprinted toward the exit as the ground shook violently beneath their feet. Cracks split along the walls, and debris from the ceiling rained down as the building began to collapse.

As they reached safety outside, a thunderous explosion ripped the night sky behind them, illuminating everything in a flash of incandescent light for a few seconds.

"Is everyone okay?" Chloe asked, catching her breath and scanning the group.

Seraphine nodded, her face pale. "We're fine. But I'm pretty sure Dr. Anaya isn't finished. She'll be back—stronger probably. That's what The Society always do."

Chloe squared her shoulders. "Then we'll be ready."

Chapter 25

A New Ally and the Hidden Room

The safehouse was tense as the team worked in small groups. Mei and Arthur huddled over the casket, their notes and diagrams spread across the table, while Yuki tinkered with a dismantled surveillance device, her sharp eyes scanning each component. Aoife sat in a corner, flipping through an old book on geospatial markings, her thick notebook beside her already half-filled with sketches. Thalia leaned against the wall, her gaze calm yet observant as she sharpened a small blade.

Chloe broke the silence, her voice steady but reflective. "Our grandmother always said the truth was like a diamond—you have to chip away the dirt to see its brilliance. She believed that even when it was hard, we had to dig deeper."

Lily smiled faintly from her seat at the window. "She used to tell me that as well. She'd say that the hardest truths are the ones worth discovering. That's why we can't stop now—we're so close."

Before anyone could respond, a sharp knock at the door broke the stillness.

Everyone froze.

Seraphine, her blade already in hand, signaled for silence and moved toward the door with careful, practiced steps. Her eyes flicked to Thalia, who joined her, her hand hovering over the pistol at her side.

Yuki swiftly killed the lights, plunging the room into shadow.

Seraphine cracked open the door slightly, enough to see an older man with weathered features, a leather satchel slung over his shoulder, and a look of cautious urgency.

"I'm Dr. Elias Crawford," he said before Seraphine could ask, his voice steady despite his unkempt appearance. "And I believe I have something you need."

Meeting Dr. Elias Crawford

The group exchanged cautious glances. Chloe gestured to Seraphine to let him in, then stepped forward, her hand poised above her holster. "Who are you, and how did you track us down?"

Dr. Crawford raised his hands in a gesture of peace. "I've been tracking The Society for years, working to stop them, and as a result, been following your own movements for some time. After your encounter at the Olive House, I realized you weren't aligned with The Society. I followed you here, as now I believe we can help each other."

Yuki crossed her arms, her tone sharp. "Or you could be leading them straight to us."

Crawford sighed as he walked over and set his satchel on the table, pulling out a collection of maps, photos, and journals. "If I wanted to harm you, would I bring all this?" he asked, spreading the materials out. "I know what they're planning—and I know how to stop them."

Aoife immediately leaned over to scrutinize the maps, her brow furrowing. "These markings look familiar. They're similar to the energy alignments I've been researching. You're mapping ley lines, aren't you?"

Crawford nodded. "Exactly. The Society is using these natural energy channels to enhance the Eye's power. If they activate the hidden room beneath the Madonna of the Trail, they will control more than just energy; they will control everything."

The Hidden Room

Chloe picked up a photograph of the Madonna of the Trail monument, its base marked with red ink. "We've been there," she said. "There's a chamber underneath, but it didn't look like this."

"That's because the room you discovered is a decoy," Crawford explained. "A more important chamber is concealed deeper. Only a select few know how to reach it."

Thalia, her dark eyes keen, leaned in closer. "Why conceal it in the first place?"

"To protect the mechanism," Crawford replied. "The Eye's amplification system was never intended to be used this way. The Society aims to harness its power to dominate resources, governments—even people. If they succeed, there will be no stopping them."

Gil frowned and crossed his arms. "How do you know all this?"

Crawford's expression softened, shadows of regret crossing his face. "Because I was once part of The Society. Decades ago, I believed in their mission—to protect knowledge for the greater good. But when I learned the truth, I left. I took everything I could to slow them down, including the plans for the hidden chamber. Since then, I've been working to undo their damage."

Mei flipped through the journal that Crawford had brought, her voice filled with excitement. "These diagrams match the inscriptions we found on the fragments!"

Arthur leaned closer to her shoulder. "This might be the important piece we need to understand how the chamber functions."

The Team's Debate

Yuki still appeared skeptical. "So now you're just here to help us out of the kindness of your heart?"

Crawford met her gaze steadily. "Call it what you like, but if I were still part of The Society, why would I bring you all this?" He gestured to the detailed maps and diagrams.

Thalia tilted her head, studying Crawford intently. "He has a point. But if you're lying, you won't get a second chance."

Chloe took a deep breath, her mind racing. "We can't afford to doubt him. If he's telling the truth, we need to act now."

Gil nodded. "If this is real, we can't let The Society get to the chamber first. But we'll need a solid plan."

Planning the Next Move

The team gathered around the table, poring over Crawford's notes. Chloe stood at the center, her voice calm yet firm. "We're heading to the Madonna of the Trail. If there's a hidden room, we'll find it—and prevent The Society from activating it."

Aoife traced the ley lines on the map. "These alignments—they converge near the monument. That's why it's crucial. If they tap into this energy point, it could exponentially amplify the Eye's power."

Chloe glanced at the team. "They'll have guards. It won't be easy."

"That's why we divide and conquer," Gil said. "Yuki and Luca, stay here to monitor communications. Mei and Arthur, continue analyzing the artifact and the inscriptions. Dr. Crawford, you're coming with me, along with Chloe, Seraphine, Aoife, and Thalia. We'll locate the chamber and shut it down."

Yuki turned to Luca. "Check our feeds. If The Society is already at the site, we need to know now."

Luca worked quickly, his fingers moving over his keyboard. A moment later, his expression tightened. "There's movement near the monument. It looks like the Society is already there."

Lily, who had been sitting quietly, stood up. Her voice steady, she declared, "Grandma always said the truth is worth fighting for. We're ready."

Crawford's expression softened. "Your grandmother must have been an amazing woman. I can see her strength in all of you."

Chloe let out a small smile. "She taught us to never back down. And we won't."

Time to Go

While the team busily sorted through, prepped and packed their gear, Chloe found herself gazing out the window into the tangled overgrowth surrounding the safehouse. She knew how important this new mission was and her determination flared up even more fiercely.

"You okay?" Gil asked, stepping beside her.

"I'm fine," Chloe replied, her voice steady. "Just thinking about what's at stake."

Gil placed a hand on her shoulder, providing silent reassurance. "We can handle this."

Before Chloe could answer, Luca's voice crackled over the comms. "There's movement near the monument. The Society's already there."

Chloe turned to the group, her voice strong and determined. "Let's go."

The Best Sausages
New York
New York
HOT DOG THE BEST
HOT DOG SAUSAGE
MADONNA OF THE TRAIL
N·S·D·A·R·MEMORIAL
PIONEER MOTHERS
COVERED WAGON DAYS

Chapter 26

More Hidden Secrets

The warm afternoon sun bathed the Madonna of the Trail monument in a golden glow, making it seem like a peaceful guardian over the bustling festival around her. Families laughed, balloons floated in the breeze, and the scent of hot dogs and kettle corn filled the air. The cheerful scene appeared perfect—except Chloe knew better.

Chloe leaned against the parked van, binoculars in hand. "They're hiding in plain sight," she said softly, her keen eyes scanning the crowd.

Gil, standing next to her with his arms crossed, nodded. "Classic move. Distract the public with fun while they execute their plan."

Inside the van, Luca and Yuki worked side by side, their screens illuminated with surveillance feeds. Yuki pointed to one monitor. "By the stage—the two suits …

they're trying too hard to appear casual. They are definitely Society agents."

"And they're busy," Luca added, tapping his tablet. "Their earpieces aren't just for show. They're coordinating something significant."

"Can you make it so we can hear what they're saying?" Yuki asked.

"Already on it."

Dr. Crawford adjusted his satchel, his expression calm but completely focused. "The real room beneath the monument won't remain hidden for much longer. If they're this active, it means they're nearing its activation."

Splitting Up

Chloe faced the team, her voice steady. "So we're splitting up. Yuki and Luca, stay here and monitor the feeds. If anything changes, you'll be our eyes and ears."

Yuki nodded. "We'll jam their comms when the time comes."

"Dr. Crawford, Gil, and I will go in to find the hidden chamber," Chloe continued.

"What about me?" Lily asked, stepping forward, determination in her eyes.

Chloe paused, then softened her tone. "You'll stay here with Mei, Arthur, Aoife, and Thalia. We need someone to coordinate and be ready to analyze anything we send back."

Lily frowned but nodded. "Fine. Just don't do anything reckless."

"We'll be fine," Chloe said with a small smile. "Promise."

The Festival's Facade

The festival was in full swing, filled with cheerful music and the hum of happy voices. Chloe, Gil, and Dr. Crawford wove through the crowd, making sure to blend in.

"It's almost too perfect," Chloe murmured, her eyes scanning the faces around her. Families enjoying ice cream, vendors selling handmade crafts—yet something felt off.

"Over there," Gil whispered, cocking his head to the right. Near the stage, a woman in a sharp suit gestured with a quick nod to someone in the crowd. "She's definitely in charge."

Dr. Crawford subtly gestured toward the monument. "The access point is at the base, hidden by a seam. We need to move quickly."

As they approached the monument, Chloe recognized a familiar face—a local shopkeeper who had always been kind to her and Lily. However, now he stood near one of the agents, his expression serious as he nodded to their commands.

Chloe's heart sank. "He's working with them, I know him, I can't believe it," she whispered. Just how far had The Society embedded themselves in her once familiar town?

Finding the Hidden Staircase

At the base of the monument, Gil knelt and traced his fingers over the carvings. "These are pressure plates. Dr. Crawford, you wouldn't happen to know what the sequence is?"

Dr. Crawford leaned closer, studying the symbols. "It's encoded in this section. Just a moment."

Chloe stood on guard, her nerves frayed as she observed the shopkeeper approaching. His once-friendly smile had turned into a cold, calculating glare.

"Chloe," he said, his tone sharp. "What are you doing here?"

Chloe forced a smile. "Just enjoying the festival."

His eyes narrowed. "Don't lie to me. The Society knows you're here. They always know."

Before she could reply, Gil pressed the last plate, and the monument rumbled. A concealed staircase slid open.

"We're in," Gil said.

The shopkeeper raised his hand, signaling nearby agents. "Not so fast."

"Run!" Chloe shouted, grabbing Dr. Crawford's arm as they darted down the stairs.

The Hidden Chamber

The narrow staircase led to a cold, damp corridor. Its stone walls were lined with faintly glowing, etched carvings. The sound of pursuit echoed behind them as they pushed forward.

"This way," Dr. Crawford said, his voice steady despite the urgent rush.

They entered a large chamber, its walls covered in intricate symbols that seemed to hum with energy. At the center stood a sleek device, glowing faintly. At the opposite end was another large door.

"This is it," Dr. Crawford said, stepping forward. "The amplification device."

Gil pushed a heavy stone slab against the door. "This won't hold them for long. Whatever you're doing, do it quickly."

Dr. Crawford examined the device, his hands swiftly navigating the controls. "I can disable it temporarily, but it won't last forever."

"Do it," Chloe said firmly. "We'll figure out the rest later."

The Society Closes In

The sound of hammering filled the air as the agents worked to get the door open. Dust and small stones rained down from the ceiling as the walls trembled.

Yuki's voice crackled through Chloe's earpiece. "Chloe, you've got a problem. The Society is redirecting their agents—everyone and their uncle is converging on you."

Chloe's stomach tightened. "Tell Luca to start the disruption. We need time."

Dr. Crawford straightened, beads of sweat forming on his brow. "The device is offline for now, but we need to leave before they get inside."

The barricaded door creaked under the weight of the agents' assault. Chloe glanced at Gil, her voice steady. "Let's go."

"Which way do we go? Agents are waiting for us up those stairs." Gill yelled.

"Here," Dr. Crawford said, gesturing toward an obscure panel near the far side door.

Lily's voice came through the earpiece, frantic. "I don't mean to alarm you but they're everywhere, Chloe. What should we do?"

Chloe gritted her teeth, her eyes scanning the chamber. "We stick to the plan. Let's meet at the fallback point. We've found a way to get out of here."

Chapter 27

Discovering the Hidden Chamber

The air grew colder and thinner as Chloe, Gil, and Dr. Crawford descended further into the next secret corridor, out of the chamber. Gil's flashlight's faint beam bounced off the ancient stone walls, creating long, eerie shadows.

From above, the distant sounds of the festival blended with sharp cries and footsteps—The Society wasn't far behind. Chloe glanced back, her heart thudding as the echoes drew nearer.

"How much farther is it, Dr. Crawford?" she asked, trying to control the tremor welling up in her voice.

The historian paused, running his hand along the wall and tracing faint carvings with his fingertips. "Not far," he murmured. "If my readings are accurate, the next chamber is just ahead."

Gil snorted lightly, adjusting the strap of his bag. "Readings? Great. Just what we need—guesswork." Despite his words, the grin on his face lightened the tension.

Chloe rolled her eyes but couldn't resist a small smile. "Focus, Gil. Let's not make this one of your comedy shows."

The Hidden Entrance

The narrow tunnel led into a small, domed room. Pale, glowing symbols shimmered on the walls, casting a warm, golden light. The air felt alive, humming with an almost magnetic energy.

Chloe gasped softly. The intricate carvings glowed more brightly as they entered the space. "It's as if the walls are breathing," she murmured.

In the center of the room stood a pedestal surrounded by concentric rings, each resembling interlocking gears.

Dr. Crawford approached the pedestal, his hands reverently gliding over its surface. "This is it," he whispered. "The key to the true chamber."

Chloe's stomach fluttered with nerves. "Do you know how to operate it?"

Dr. Crawford examined the grooves closely. "Yes, but it's fragile. One wrong move, and the mechanism will reset. We'll lose our opportunity."

Gil approached the entrance, his flashlight sweeping over the corridor. "In other words—don't mess it up," he teased with a wink.

"Helpful as always," Chloe said dryly, crossing her arms.

Revealing the Chamber

As Dr. Crawford aligned the artifact, the gears started to spin, their rhythmic clicking increasing in volume. The glowing symbols on the walls brightened, filling the room with a golden light that pulsed in sync with the hum of the pedestal.

With a final, resonant click, the pedestal sank into the floor. A concealed door slid open nearby, revealing a vast chamber filled with glowing pillars and intricate carvings.

Chloe stepped inside, her eyes widening in awe. "This ... this is incredible."

The room was breathtaking. Towering stone columns stretched toward a domed ceiling adorned with shimmering symbols, each one shifting like stars in the night sky. At the center of the room stood a crystalline structure, glowing with a soft, pulsating light that seemed to resonate with the very air.

Dr. Crawford spoke softly, a respectful reverence in his tone, saying, "Welcome to the amplification core—the heart and soul of the Eye's incredible power."

Chloe's heart raced as she turned to him. "Can we destroy it?"

Dr. Crawford shook his head. "Not without destabilizing the other nodes connected to it. But I can deactivate it as well—for now."

The Society Closes In

Before they could act, the distant sound of heavy footsteps echoed through the corridor.

"They're coming," Gil announced, stepping toward the entrance. His face was calm, but his body taut, his stance prepared for action. "We don't have much time."

Chloe picked up her earpiece. "Yuki, what's the status?"

Yuki's voice crackled through. "We've jammed their communications for now, but their reinforcements are moving quickly. You need to hurry."

Chloe turned to Dr. Crawford and asked, "How long will it take to shut this down?"

"About ten minutes," he said, already examining the core.

"You've got five," Chloe replied, pulling her weapon.

The Fight Begins

The first wave of Society agents flooded into the corridor leading towards the room, their shadows stretching in front of them.

"Here we go," Gil murmured, clutching his weapon tightly.

The air erupted in noise as the agents charged. Gil sent warning shots down the corridor, forcing them to slow their advance. Chloe fired alongside him, her hands steady even as her heart raced.

"More are on the way!" Gil shouted, throwing Chloe a flash grenade.

She grabbed it, pulled the pin, and threw it into the corridor. Blinding light and a deafening explosion resonated through the chamber, stopping the agents in their tracks—temporarily.

"Dr. Crawford, how's it going?" Chloe shouted.

"Almost there!" he called back, his fingers flying over the controls.

Disabling the Core

The glowing core started to fade, its pulsating light diminishing to a faint flicker. Dr. Crawford stepped back, sweat beading on his forehead. "It's done! The core is disabled—but only for now. We need to move before they get to us."

Chloe glanced down the corridor, still filled with smoke, and where the agents were still lying knocked flat by the grenade. "Then let's go!"

A Narrow Escape

The trio sprinted past the dazed, fallen agents who didn't even notice them, up the way they had come. Faint sounds of shouts and breaking stone echoed behind them. As they burst into the sunlight, the chaos of the festival welcomed them once more—cheering crowds oblivious to the danger just beneath their feet.

Yuki and Luca pulled up nearby in the van with its back doors open. "Get in!" Yuki shouted, beckoning them to hurry.

Chloe, Gil, and Dr. Crawford tumbled inside as the van roared to life. Through the rear window, they watched Society agents pour out of the monument, their frustration clear even from a distance.

That was a Close One

In the van, Chloe leaned forward, trying to catch her breath. "How long do we have before they reactivate it?"

Dr. Crawford's expression was serious. "It could be hours, maybe less. They'll regroup quickly."

Lily's voice came through the comms. "What's next, Chloe?"

Chloe gazed out the window, her blue eyes blazing. "I'm not sure, but I do know we'll work it out. We will stop them."

Chapter 28

Preparing for the Final Takedown

Back at the safehouse, everyone gathered around the old wooden table. Maps, gadgets, and notebooks cluttered the surface, and the faint glow of a laptop illuminated Yuki's focused face. The team was preparing for the biggest mission yet, and the air buzzed with a mix of nervous energy and steely resolve.

Yuki tapped her laptop screen, drawing everyone's attention. "I've intercepted more of The Society's plans," she said, her voice steady yet serious. "They're heading to Mt. Baldy. That's where they'll activate the Eye."

Luca leaned over her shoulder, gazing at the screen. "Classic villain move. Remote mountain base, advanced tech, and a world domination plan. All they're missing is a volcano."

Despite the tension, Lily giggled, receiving a playful

playful nudge from Chloe. "Focus, Luca," Chloe said, although a faint smile tugged at her lips.

"They've installed motion sensors and drones around the perimeter," Yuki replied. "I can disable the sensors from a distance, but the drones are more complicated. They move randomly, so we'll need to stay alert."

"I've got that covered," Luca said, grinning as he cracked his knuckles. "I've been working on a little program to interfere with their drone signals. It won't last long, but it'll give us a chance."

Lily raised her hand, her voice steady. "What about inside? What's waiting for us?"

Gil's expression grew serious. "We don't know. The Society has been secretive about the core setup. We'll need to adapt once we're in."

Seraphine, seated quietly in the corner, finally spoke. "They'll have multiple layers of defense—redundancies, hidden guards, and automated systems. The Society never leaves anything unprotected."

Chloe turned to her, her eyes sharp. "How do you know?"

Seraphine paused for a moment, then sighed. "Because I helped design some of those systems before I left them."

The room went silent, the implication of her words settling over the group.

Aoife broke the silence, her Irish accent gentle yet confident. "Then it's a good thing you're with us now. You'll know how to defeat them."

Seraphine gave a small nod, the corners of her mouth lifting into a rare smile. "Let's hope so."

Planning the Penetration

Gil laid out a detailed map of Mt. Baldy on the table, highlighting a lush, wooded area close to the summit. "This is where their base is. The terrain is a bit challenging—lots of trees, rocky paths, and steep climbs. While it gives them a significant advantage, we can definitely turn it in our favor as well!"

Aoife leaned over the map, her tall frame casting a shadow over the table. "The natural terrain could be their weakness. I can guide us through the less obvious paths—ones they might miss."

Yuki nodded. "Good. The more unexpected our approach, the better."

"Let's split into two teams," Chloe said, taking the lead. "Yuki, Luca, and Thalia can manage surveillance and sabotage their systems. Aoife, Gil, Seraphine, and I will penetrate the base."

"And … *what about me?*" Lily asked, her voice quiet but firm.

Chloe turned to her younger sister. "You'll stay here with Mei and Arthur. If anything goes wrong, we'll need you to help with analyzing everything we transmit back."

Lily's expression grew tense. "Again."

Chloe shrugged, "We need everyone contributing in some way, Lily and nothing any of us do is insignificant. You've been invaluable doing that so far!"

"Fine," Lily retorted, rolling her eyes.

"Hey, we'll all be careful," Chloe said, her voice softening. "That's how we win."

Individual Moments

As the team worked through the rest of the day and late into the night, they broke into their individual groups, and little moments of connection sprang up between them.

Chloe and Gil

Chloe stood by the window, gazing out at the moonlit street. Her shoulders were tense, and her mind raced under the weight of the leadership role she had seemed to grow into with this team.

Gil leaned casually against the wall beside her. "You know, you're doing great," he said in a low voice.

She glanced at him, a wry smile on her face. "Does it look that way? Because it sure doesn't feel that way."

"You brought us together," he said simply. "That counts for something."

She sighed. "I just don't want to lose anyone else."

Gil's gaze softened. "We've got your back, Chloe. We all do. Trust us to do our part."

She smiled softly. "Thanks, Gil."

Yuki and Luca

At the table, Yuki was intensely focused on her laptop, her fingers dancing across the keyboard. Luca sat beside her, twirling a pen between his fingers.

"You're going to fry your brain," Luca teased, leaning back in his chair.

Yuki gave him a brief glare. "If I don't, we'll all be walking into a death trap."

"Fair point," he said, raising his hands. "But maybe you should take a break before you accidentally hack a toaster."

Yuki smirked, a rare spark of fun interrupting her focus. "I'll keep that in mind."

Seraphine and Mei

Seraphine sat away from the group, sharpening her blade with slow, deliberate motions. Mei approached her, hesitating before she spoke.

"Are you okay?" Mei asked gently.

Seraphine looked up, her eyes thoughtful. "I'm fine."

"You don't have to do this alone," Mei said, her tone kind but firm. "We're all in this together."

Seraphine's lips twitched into a faint smile. "Thanks, Mei."

Setting Out

As the team packed their gear, the weight of the mission was pressing, but their determination remained unshaken.

Yuki gave Chloe a small device. "This will temporarily jam their communications. Use it wisely."

"Got it," Chloe said, tucking it into her bag.

Arthur glanced up from his notes. "We'll keep an eye on everything from here. If anything changes, we'll inform you right away."

Chloe nodded. "Thank you. We'll make it count."

Off to Mt. Baldy

The drive to Mt. Baldy was quiet, and the van was filled with tense, focused energy. As the mountain came into view, its jagged silhouette etched against the early dawn, Chloe took a deep breath. It looked terribly imposing.

"This is it," she said, once they'd stopped, stepping out into the crisp mountain air.

Gil joined her, his dark eyes scanning the horizon. "Ready?"

Chloe nodded, her voice steady. "Let's finish this."

The team slipped into the shadows of the trees, their steps silent yet determined. Above them, the mountain loomed like a final, daunting challenge, waiting for them to rise to the occasion.

Chapter 29

The Battle at Mt. Baldy

The morning sunlight filtered softly through the towering pines as the team crouched in the shadows of the forest. The crisp scent of damp earth and pine needles filled the air, but the peaceful surroundings clashed with the tension that hung over them. The hum of drones buzzed faintly in the distance, reminding them of the danger that was ahead.

Chloe adjusted her earpiece, her blue eyes locked on the heavily guarded base nestled into the rocky side of Mt. Baldy's summit. The Society's sharp-edged, metallic structures glinted menacingly in the sunlight. Equipment pulsed faintly with an eerie green glow, looking out of place in the mountain's otherwise natural beauty.

Yuki's voice crackled in their ears, calm but concise. "Drones are circling every five minutes. I've temporarily disabled their motion sensors, but you need to move quickly. This window won't last long."

Gil glanced at his watch, his dark eyes unwavering. "We have one chance. Let's make it count."

Chloe turned to the group. "Team One is with me—Gil and Seraphine. Team Two, hold back and create a diversion when we signal."

Entering the Belly of the Beast

Chloe, Gil, and Seraphine quietly moved through the trees, their footsteps muffled by the soft forest floor. As they neared the base, the hum of machinery became louder, blending with the distant voices of agents barking orders.

At the edge of the base, Seraphine knelt by a hidden access panel set into the rock. Her hands moved quickly, her actions precise and confident. "This is one of the backup systems I designed," she said quietly, a flicker of guilt in her voice. "I can override it, but we'll only have a few minutes, at best, before they notice."

"Then don't waste time," Chloe said, her weapon ready as she scanned the area.

After a soft beep, the panel slid open, revealing a narrow passage. The group slipped inside, keeping to the shadows, moving silently through the complex, until they were approaching the glowing core at the center of the base. Thick cables snaked across the ground, connecting the core to monitors and machinery.

Seraphine stared at the mechanism, her expression grim. "It's worse than I expected. They're closer to activation than I thought."

The Activation Mechanism

Arthur's voice chimed through their earpieces, steady but urgent. "That's the amplification core. If they complete the sequence, the Eye's power will sync with their global network. Then it's game over."

Chloe's jaw tightened. "Seraphine, can you shut it down?"

Seraphine hesitated, her green eyes narrowing as she examined the system. "I can try, but there are redundancies. The only way to end this for good is to destroy the main core."

Before she could move, a voice echoed behind them, dripping with arrogance. "Well, well. Look who decided to crash the party."

Chloe spun around, her heart pounding. Dr. Anaya stood at the edge of the platform, flanked by two agents armed to the teeth. Her sharp features were twisted in a smug smile.

"You just don't know when to quit, do you?" Dr. Anaya taunted. "But it doesn't matter. The Eye's power will reshape the world—and there's nothing you can do to stop it."

The Battle Begins

Gunfire erupted, shattering the standoff. Chloe and Gil dove behind cover, firing back as Seraphine rushed to a nearby control panel, her fingers flying over the keys in an effort to disrupt the sequence.

"Yuki, we need that diversion now!" Chloe shouted into her comms.

"On it!" Yuki replied, her voice steady.

Moments later, explosions shook the far side of the base. Drones spun out of control, crashing into equipment, while flames shot into the sky. Smoke billowed, sending the agents into chaos.

Some agents disappeared, probably running to see what had just happened, while others kept up sporadically firing, trying to stop Seraphine but missing.

Gil provided cover fire, moving confidently and precisely. "Chloe, go! I'll keep them busy!"

Chloe sprinted toward the core, her heart pounding as the green light brightened, enveloping the platform in an otherworldly glow.

"Arthur," she shouted, "how much time do we have?"

Arthur's reply was clipped. "Not enough. The sequence is almost complete."

The Eye's Fragment Activates

As Chloe reached the core, a surge of energy rippled through the air, knocking her off balance. Inside a containment unit, a fragment of the Eye glowed even brighter, arcs of electricity snapping across the room like a storm.

"Seraphine, there's no more time, move!" she shouted.

"Chloe, fall back!" Gil called frantically.

Ignoring him, Chloe stumbled forward and planted an explosive charge at the base of the core, her hands trembling but steady. Before she could finish, Dr. Anaya's mocking laughter echoed once more.

"Destroy it if you want," Dr. Anaya sneered as she grabbed the fragment inside the containment unit. "You've already lost."

She rushed toward an escape route, the fragment clutched tightly in her hands.

"Stop her!" Chloe shouted, but another burst of energy from the core pushed her and Gil back.

A Narrow Escape

Seraphine joined Gil and Chloe at the edge of the platform, her face pale yet resolute. "If that core explodes, it will take down the entire base with it. We need to leave. Now."

Gil hesitated, his eyes blazing. "We can't let Dr. Anaya escape!"

Chloe placed a firm hand on his arm. "We'll stop her. But if we die here, this fight ends."

Reluctantly, Gil nodded, and the group sprinted toward the exit as the core's hum reached a deafening crescendo, sparking, coiling ropes of electric arcs filled the room.

The Explosion

The team had barely reached the tree line before the core exploded. The shockwave knocked them to the ground, and a column of fire shot into the sky.

The air swirled thick with the acrid stench of burning metal and smoke, and the mountain trembled beneath them.

Chloe lay on her back, gasping for breath. Around her, the others struggled to their feet, dust and debris clinging to their clothes.

"Is everyone okay?" she asked, her voice hoarse.

"We're fine," Yuki said, brushing soot off her jacket. "But Dr. Anaya escaped with the fragment."

Chloe clenched her fists, her eyes blazing as she stared at the smoking ruins. "This isn't over."

Aftermath

The group huddled together, battered but alive, their faces reflecting the turmoil they felt—relief, anger, determination, frustration.

"How much damage did we do?" Chloe asked Dr. Crawford through comms.

"Enough to slow them down," he said grimly. "But with that fragment, they'll regroup—and they'll be even more dangerous."

Chloe straightened, her gaze steady. "Then we'll be ready. They won't win. Not while we're still standing."

As the smoke from the explosion curled into the morning sky, the team turned to the mountain path, ready to face whatever came next.

Chapter 30

Planning the Next Mission

Gil laid out a detailed map of Jerusalem, its winding streets, and historic landmarks marked with notes. "Israel is definitely next, we know that now. The Society will probably target the Seven Seals, but let's try get confirmation on that—I saw a parchment scroll in that one chamber that may be just what we need," he said, his voice steady as his finger traced the area. "It's a risk but we can dash back there and retrieve it. For sure, if they intend to use the seals, they'll need to find them, probably somewhere below the city—possibly ancient ruins."

Chloe nodded, her eyes scanning the map. "That's where they'll have their defenses. If we're going to stop them, we'll need a team capable of navigating those ruins and understanding what they're looking for."

Aoife leaned in, her hands gently turning the pages

of a notebook brimming with her geospatial sketches. "If they use the underground infrastructure, I can accurately identify the precise locations. The layers of Jerusalem unveil its rich history—I'll bet I can discover where they're concealed!"

Thalia, sitting across the table, adjusted her glasses and smirked. "And if there's anything written in cryptic symbols or forgotten languages, I'll be there to decipher it. I've been waiting for something like this."

Gil glanced at her, his lips curling into a slight smile. "Just be quick. The Society isn't going to give us much time."

Chloe folded her arms, her expression firm. "So, it's decided. Gil will lead the mission since it's in Israel. We'll all go: Seraphine, Aoife, Yuki, Lily, Mei, Luca, and Thalia. All except Arthur, who will stay here to monitor and provide support."

Setting the Stage for Israel

As the team continued their preparations, the tension in the safehouse began to ease slightly. Yuki handed Chloe a secure tablet loaded with maps and data. "This contains everything we've gathered so far. If The

Society uses ancient ruins, it's likely connected to the Old City."

Chloe, with her sharp wit and a thirst for knowledge, took the tablet eagerly. "I'll cross-reference this with the encrypted data we intercepted. If there's a pattern, I'll find it." Her mind was racing, sorting through potential connections and vulnerabilities The Society might have overlooked.

Arthur spoke from the corner, his voice calm yet thoughtful. "Thalia's expertise will be invaluable if they tap into old systems or cryptic mechanisms. The Society is not just after power—they seek control rooted in history. Don't underestimate their knowledge."

Thalia grinned as she flipped through one of Arthur's old journals. "They can't know everything. Whatever they've left behind, I'll figure it out. Cryptography and ancient languages are my playground." Her skills in deciphering codes and cracking hidden messages would be critical in uncovering The Society's hidden pathways.

Gil leaned against the wall, adjusting the strap of his bag. A former Israeli special forces operative, his sharp brown eyes scanned the group. "Aoife will ensure we don't get lost along the way."

Aoife chuckled softly, her Irish accent warm. "Don't worry. I'll get you where you need to go. Don't blame me if we have to squeeze through a few tight spaces." As a geospatial analyst with a background in geology, her understanding of underground structures and natural terrain would be key in navigating the labyrinthine paths they might face.

Seraphine's voice was low but resolute. "I know The Society's methods. If they're after the Seven Seals, and I agree, I suspect they are, I'll know how to anticipate their moves." With her deep knowledge of The Society's tactics and history, she was their best chance at staying one step ahead.

Luca, being their cybersecurity expert, smirked as he tapped away on his laptop. "If The Society has a digital lock, I'll find the key. Firewalls, surveillance feeds—if they rely on technology, they're already compromised." His ability to infiltrate systems and override security measures would be crucial for gathering intelligence and ensuring their movements remained undetected.

Across the room, Mei meticulously checked the supplies she had brought. As a biologist and chemist, she specialized in synthetic compounds. "If The Society is tampering with ancient artifacts, I'll be able to tell what they're doing and whether we should be worried."

Yuki, as their robotics and nanotechnology specialist, added. "And if we need a bypass, I have just the tools for it." Her precision engineering skills had already saved them more than once, and they would undoubtedly be needed again.

Lily, ever the writer with a knack for uncovering secrets and a love for the dramatic, meticulously checked the contents of her backpack. She had stocked it with essential supplies—first aid, compact survival tools, and a small notebook filled with her own observations. She glanced at Chloe, determination flashing in her eyes. "I know I'm not an expert like the rest of you, but I'll be ready for whatever comes. I've been studying the case files and memorized every detail we have on The Society's movements."

Chloe gave her a proud smile. "You don't have to be an expert, Lily. Your instincts and quick thinking have already proven invaluable."

Lily zipped up her bag, her expression resolute. "Then let's make it count."

The Next Mission Begins

As the final preparations were made, the team gathered at the safehouse entrance where Arthur stood, his hands resting on his cane. The weight of years and wisdom settled in his gaze as he looked at each of them, his expression a mixture of pride and concern.

"You all know what you're up against," he said, his voice steady but rich with emotion. "This mission isn't just about history or artifacts. It's about protecting something far greater than any of us. Stay sharp, stay together."

Chloe stepped forward first, her blue eyes filled with appreciation. "We wouldn't have made it this far without you, Arthur. Thank you for everything."

He gave her a small smile. "You remind me of myself when I was young—too stubborn for your own good. That's not a bad thing. Just don't let it get you into trouble."

Lily hugged him next, gripping him tightly. "You always believed in us, even when no one else did."

"I still do," Arthur replied, his voice softer now. "Now go prove me right."

Gil shook his hand, a firm, respectful grip between two men who understood the cost of battles fought in the shadows. "We'll keep you updated as much as we can."

Arthur nodded. "Just don't get yourselves killed. I'm too old to start training a new group."

The others said their goodbyes in turn—Thalia with a wink, Luca with a playful salute, Yuki and Mei with quiet bows of respect, Aoife with a firm clap on the shoulder, and Seraphine with a rare, knowing smile.

The team climbed into the waiting vehicles with their bags packed and their hearts set on the task ahead. Arthur remained at the door as they pulled away, watching them disappear to the distance. He exhaled slowly, his grip tightening on his cane.

"Their story is just beginning," he murmured to himself. "Godspeed."

Having retrieved the important parchment safely, the team arrived at the airport and moved through security with silent determination. No second thoughts, no hesitation—only the unshakable bond that tied them together. As they boarded their flight, a sense of purpose filled the air. The mission had begun.

The Society

In a dimly lit room, Dr. Anaya stood before a map of Jerusalem, glowing in the light of the fragment of the Eye which pulsed with a steady rhythm on a nearby table. It cast an eerie green light across her face.

"They're coming," she said, her tone sharp but unshaken. "Let them. They won't stop us this time."

Another figure stepped from the shadows, his voice smooth and cold. "They're resourceful, but they're only delaying the inevitable. The Dome of the Rock is the perfect site for our plans. When they arrive, they'll already be too late."

An ancient stone engraving on the wall behind them was bathed in the Eye's glow. It was adorned with intricate symbols, suggesting something even deeper beneath the surface.

To Be Continued in *The Land of Promise ...*

Thank You, Dear Readers!

Wow, what a journey this has been! Writing this story was pure joy from start to finish. Bringing Upland to life with its unique blend of real charm and a splash (okay, maybe a bucketful) of fiction was an exciting adventure for me. I truly hope you enjoyed reading it as much as I loved creating it.

Thank you for taking this ride with the amazing Sisterhood Sleuths. Their bravery, wit, and teamwork are the heart of these stories, but your imagination gives them life. It means the world to me that you chose to spend your time with them (and me)!

And the journey isn't over yet! If you're eager for more sleuthing, mystery, and adventure, stay tuned for the Sisterhood Sleuths' upcoming escapades across the globe in 2025. The entire series is as follows:

- *The Obsidian Eye (Upland, California)*
- *The Land of Promise: The Seven Seals (Israel)*
- *The Swiss Enigma: Secrets of the Alps* (Switzerland)
- *Whispers in the Catacombs: Uncovering Naples' Deep Mysteries* (Italy)

- *The Louvre Enigma: Deciphering Codes Among the Masterpieces* (France)
- *The Celtic Mask: Shadows of The Emerald Isle* (Ireland)
- *The Northern Code: Secrets of the Midnight Sun* (Iceland)
- *The Dragon's Awakening: A Tale of Ancient Secrets and Modern Threats* (Japan)

From ancient scrolls to hidden chambers, from icy landscapes to lush forests, Chloe, Lily, and the gang are ready for more mysteries—and I hope you'll join them.

Thank you for believing in this story and these characters. You've made this dream of mine come alive, and I'm forever grateful for that.

Until next time, keep your sleuthing skills sharp and your imagination sharper!

With gratitude and a smile,

Cathy Warshaw

Unlock the Secrets!

Become a part of the adventures,

join the Sisterhood Sleuths and receive thrilling

mysteries, exclusive behind-the-scenes content, and a

chance to win incredible prizes!

www.SisterhoodSleuths.net